HOW TO WRITE AND SELL EROTICA

TRICKS OF THE TRADE FROM THE GREAT LITERARY PROVOCATEURS

M. CHRISTIAN

Barbary Coast Editions
A Renaissance E Books publication
San Francisco CA
2011

www. BarbaryCoastEditions.com

ISBN 9781615083015

Manufactured in the United States of America

First Barbary Coast Editions Edition: March 2011

10 9 8 7 6 5 4 3 2 1

Cover and book design: Frankie Hill

Acknowledgment

"Ten Years in Bed with the Best: The History of ERWA" by Adrienne Benedicks originally appeared in Cream, *Best of the Erotica Readers & Writers Association*, edited by Lisabet Sarai, published by Thunder's Mouth Press, 2006.

For Jean Marie–
–a great publisher and an even greater friend

CONTENTS

INTRODUCTION I: HELLO, MY NAME IS CHRIS AND I WRITE EROTICA FOR A LIVING

I wrote my first story when I was in the fourth grade, and because I was obsessed with Jules Verne, it was all brass fittings, steam, and iron. Scared out of my tiny wits, I dropped it on my teacher's desk. She either never saw it or didn't know what to do with it or me, because she didn't say anything about it.

In high school the idea of actually trying to write—and sell what I wrote—came back. It's strange, and I can't remember exactly what happened to make it so intense, but when it returned it came with a serious, almost frightening, WHAM of dedication. On and off—though mostly on—I tried to write a story a week ... for close to ten years.

Yes, you may gasp. Sure, you can shake your head. But that's what happened. What's even worse is that I couldn't sell any of them—though I did come close a few rare times.

I also took a lot, and I mean a lot, of writing classes: expensive ones taught by professionals, cheap ones taught by amateurs, community college ones, state college ones ... and pretty much every one of them had been totally, absolutely useless. One of them was taught by a professor who—halfway thought the semester—stopped everything to announce his first published story, in a tiny magazine for bulldog enthusiasts. Another was by a kind-of-famous science fiction writer who was more interested in having his ego massaged than actually teaching anything about telling a good story. Then there were the dozens I'd been in where I was the only one seriously trying to be a professional—and everyone else was there just because they thought it was going to be an easy A.

At my wits' end, I finally enrolled in a class on writing erotica taught by Lisa Palac, who at the time edited a magazine called *FutureSex*. On a whim, I'd brought a story with me, a shot I'd taken at erotica, and nervously handed to Lisa.

She bought it. Susie Bright then picked up "Intercore" for the 1994 edition of *Best American Erotica*.

And, just like that, I was a pornographer.

Fast forward fifteen years and ... well, here I am: 300+ published short stories, six collections of short stories, editor of 20 or so anthologies, author of six novels, and so on, so forth. Many of these are erotica, but I've got lots in all kinds of other genres: horror, mystery, romance, humor, non-fiction ... but everything really started with selling that one little story about people having sex.

Through the years, I struggled to learn what it really meant to be a professional writer. I kept thinking of what I wished I'd been taught — and how, if I got the chance, I'd teach others what I wish I'd learned much earlier in my writing journey. Then Adrienne at the Erotica Readers and Writers Association site gave me that chance. I really can't say enough good things about Adrienne and the community she's built except to say that there is one — and only one — definitive resource for erotica writers, and it's ERWA. Want thoughtful and incisive reviews? ERWA. Want to chat and share war stories with other pornographers? ERWA. Want articles and essays about writing erotica? ERWA. Want to know which publishers are looking for manuscripts, and which editors need stories? ERWA.

Since 2000 or so I've been writing a mostly-monthly column for ERWA called *Confessions of a Literary Streetwalker* - whose title, by the way, comes from my running joke of being willing to write anything, for anyone, at any time; you name the kink and I'll write it for you.

What I tried to do with these columns was to finally give beginning writers the lessons I wish I'd gotten, but also to show the all-important truth about how to write good erotica.

The great folks at Renaissance E Books — about whom I also can't say enough good things — have given me an opportunity to put all the columns I've written together into this one book: my two-cent thoughts and hard-earned experiences in

+ creating interesting plots and interesting characters,
+ the tough business of being a writer,
+ sexual mistakes,
+ the four deadly sins of erotica,
+ how to talk to editors and publishers,
+ how to emotionally take care of yourself,
+ publicity tricks and advice,
+ cultivating your imagination,
+ writing for all kinds of fetishes,
+ how to write beyond your own sexual interests and orientation,
+ and much more.

Even though a few of these columns were written before the ebook revolution, I've decided to keep most of them pretty much intact — except for a few tweaks to save me some serious embarrassment — because even though we've entered a new publishing world of digital media, a lot of what I was talking about still exists, and probably will continue to exist for as long as there are stories and people to write them.

As I'm hardly the end-all-be-all expert on writing and selling erotica — my dumpster full of rejection slips proves that — I also asked a few of my pals to contribute their own opinions on erotica writing. Some of them are far better than me and a few are just starting out—but they all have their own takes on what it means to be a smut writer.

Even though I honestly think there's a lot of important information in my columns and the advice here from my friends, the most important lesson is that, when all is said and done, being a writer—of erotica or any other genre—is a very personal voyage. Yours won't be like mine, and mine won't be like yours. Take what you need, but don't think that anyone ever has all the answers.

Want to know how to write a good erotic story? The answer is the same for writing a good romance, a good mystery, a good horror, a good … well, anything story: just write a good story.

And how to do that? Well, that's what this book is all about. I hope you enjoy it and that it helps you write … whatever it is you want to write, sexy or not.

- M. Christian

INTRODUCTION II
TEN YEARS IN BED WITH THE BEST: THE HISTORY OF ERWA
ADRIENNE BENEDICKS

It's difficult to write good erotica. Authors in any fictional genre have to master the elements of the craft: plot, characterization, dialogue, and so on. Erotica authors need to go further. They need to depict sexual acts, situations, and emotions that are believable and arousing. To do this, they draw on their personal insights and images. They delve into their imaginations, lay bare their sensual fantasies, and share those visions with their readers. Authors who dare expose themselves via erotica are brave souls, indeed.

To my delight, I find myself today surrounded by these fascinating people: the writers of sexually explicit fiction. These are the people who populate the virtual world of ERWA, the world we have built together over the past ten years.

In 1996, when I first plugged into the Internet, I admit that the first thing I looked for was porn. I craved sexy stories. Much to my disappointment all I found were boring, mechanical sex scenes, and a lot of "Ohhh my Gawd, I'm cummming" nonsense. It didn't take me long to realize that much of the adult web was simply a digital form of male-oriented one-dimensional erotica, a cyber circle-jerk. I was disappointed. As a woman I felt left out of the dirty stuff.

I thought that surely I wasn't unique in my desire for well-written, hot erotic stories—real stories, not just bits and pieces of fuckscenes. So I hit the chat rooms and asked, "Where's the quality sexy stuff?" That was like plastering a blinking "Who wants to screw me?" tag on my emails. Live and learn!

For my next attempt, I joined Romance Readers Anonymous (RRA) email list. I thought that surely, romance readers would be comfortable discussing erotic stories. In those days, though, we couldn't talk about sex in our public posts, even though many romances were highly erotic.

A few of us listers took to chatting off-list about the erotic parts of romance. I suggested that we live on the edge and start our own list. Great excitement greeted my suggestion, and on June 5th, 1996, the Erotica Readers Association was born. ERA, an affectionate play on the Equal Rights Amendment, was a sister list to RRA, and the foundation of the current Erotica Readers & Writers Association.

4

At that time my children were in high school, and I had the opportunity to finish my degree in Anthropology. As a student, I had access to various online options and with the endorsement of my professor, the University agreed to host ERA email list. My goal was to provide a private, secure online space where women could comfortably discuss erotic fiction and sexuality, away from the "hey baby, what ya wearing" crowd.

Subscription was by request or invitation. Publicity worked via word of mouth. Within two months we had sixty women onboard; fabulous, fun, curious women who were eager to talk about sexy writings, and to discuss the joys, problems, or disappointments of their own sexuality.

It didn't take long before these readers decided to try their own hands at writing sexy fiction. "I bet even I can write a sex scene better that!" was a typical inspiration. We quickly learned that writing good erotica wasn't as easy as it seemed. The general assumption was that if you were capable of having sex, then surely you could write about it. Not necessarily true—but that didn't stop us from trying. We were having a lot of fun, even when our fictional efforts fell flat.

Before long, a few brave men who were friends of ERA subscribers were asking to join. They liked reading erotic stories, and they liked the idea of smart discussions about sex. So I opened the door; ERA became inclusive rather then exclusive. Most women were pleased with the change. A few stomped off the list, sure ERA would crumble into a "hey baby" chat room atmosphere.

That didn't happen. Men brought their unique sexual insight into ERA, and our horizons grew even more as people of all sexual persuasions requested subscription. ERA became a dynamic robust community of people interested in sexuality in the written word, and in their lives.

Of course, we had our fair share of narrow-minded confrontational types, rigid viewpoints, and egos too big even for the World Wide Web. Overall, though, ERAers were non-judgmental, mutually respectful and more than willing to get along.

ERA grew quickly that first year. Subscribers suggested that I start a Web site to house all the material we were accumulating: book recommendations, hints about popular authors, discussions on where to buy erotica (at that time erotica wasn't sitting on book shop shelves). A subscriber volunteered to build a site, and the domain "www.erotica-readers.com" became an on-line reality.

We decided to be really daring, and started putting subscribers' original stories behind a password protected "Green Door" on the ERA Web site. We felt so very sophisticated, and risqué, with our personal secret stash of erotica sitting right out there on the Web!

ERA continued to grow, and so did subscribers' interest in writing erotica. Writers were taking a serious interest in helping each other improve. Stories were shared on the list, and critiques and suggestions on how to improve the works were cheerfully and willingly given. ERA was evolving, moving from its readers' base to a writers' base. More and more focus was on writers helping writers.

Around this time, erotica anthologies were becoming very popular. The *Herotica* series (Down There Press) had made a big splash, leading the way to *The Best Women's Erotica* (Cleis Press), *Best American Erotica* (Simon & Schuster), *The Mammoth Book of Best New Erotica* (Carroll & Graf), *Best Lesbian Erotica* (Cleis Press), and *Ultimate Gay Erotica* (Alyson Press).

Web site magazines were springing up like grass — and weeds. There was a growing market for erotic short stories, and many ERA subscribers were ready to try publishing their work. They exposed themselves, so to speak, behind ERA's Green Door; the experience gave them confidence. With support and encouragement from their peers, ERA subscribers started to submit stories to various calls for submissions.

ERA already had a solid community feel. Subscribers really did care about each other. We were a virtual family. Even so, I was pleasantly surprised at how generous writers were in sharing calls for submissions. Rather than concealing the information to reduce the competition, ERAers said: "Hey everybody, look what I found! Let's give it a try."

At that time, the ERA Web site was still a small dot in the adult web, but there was no doubt our growing resources and stash of sexy stories was drawing in a smart crowd. I took the plunge, and with a lot of help and suggestions from the community, gave the ERA site a new look that was sensual and classy, as well as easy to navigate.

I didn't realize the obvious: being out in the Web made my private email list, nicely hidden and hosted by the University computer center, suddenly quite visible. Subscription was still by request or invitation, but now inquiries came pouring in. People landing on ERA Web site liked the resources they found there, and wanted to know more. Subscriptions grew, the site grew, and soon ERA was pulling in more then 13% of the university web traffic. ERA had to go, they told me, and gave me two weeks to find another host.

Ah, the price of success! Fortunately, an Australian subscriber volunteered the help of her husband, who ran his own ISP service. Kevin hosted ERA for free for several years until we once again grew too big and had to move on to our present home, a major adult web hosting company.

By 2000 ERA had grown so large and had such a varied focus that things were getting out of hand. The sheer number of emails on the list caused confusion and havoc. Writers were frustrated in their efforts to have their stories critiqued because their works were lost in the deluge of chitchat emails. Questions and concerns about publishing and marketing went unanswered because busy subscribers didn't have time or patience to dig through hundreds of emails, and were simply deleting it all. Meanwhile the amount of information on the site was overwhelming. The organization was on the verge of losing itself in too much of everything. It would have been an ironic death by popularity. At this point I understood that ERA was no long a simple hobby. Good erotica had become a worthy pursuit. Erotica readers were hungry for the good stuff, and publishers were geared up to provide it. I wanted the ERA Web site to be *the place* where erotica readers and writers would come for the information they needed and where editors and publishers would come when looking for talented writers. I wanted ERA to be the premier Web site for quality erotica. Finally, I wanted to continue to provide an email list where erotica readers and writers could network, and where people could comfortably discuss sexuality.

The first step was to change the Erotica Readers Association name to better reflect what we had become: the Erotica Readers & Writers Association (ERWA). The second step was to create a flexible infrastructure for the site and for the email list, a foundation with enough latitude for future changes. Here's where ERWA subscribers came to the rescue, once again. Suggestions poured in, and I followed through. The evolution of ERWA was, and I suspect always will be, a community affair.

ERWA became three distinct parts that made up the whole: ERWA email discussion list, ERWA Web site, and the humorous and informative ERWA monthly newsletter, *Erotic Lure*, currently written by Lisabet Sarai.

The ERWA Web site retained its basic design. The richness and utility of the site grew as publishers and editors recognized ERWA's potential. No longer did I spend hours searching for viable markets. Calls for submissions now came to me.

ERWA's story galleries became a source of quality erotic fiction. Editors routinely mined the galleries' content for their "Best Of" erotic anthologies. Renowned erotic authors came on board as columnists, providing advice in our Authors Resources section. The luminaries of the adult literary world offered provocative articles on hot sexual topics in the Smutter's Lounge pages.

I divided ERWA email discussion list into four opt-in sections; Admin (for news related to ERWA, calls for submissions, events, and other items of interest); Parlor (an open forum with a social ambiance); Writers (dedicated to authorship and related issues); and Storytime (an informal writers' workshop where authors share their stories for comments and critiques). The very best of Storytime works are placed in ERWA Erotica Galleries.

Currently, The Erotica Readers & Writers Association hosts an email discussion list of over 1200 subscribers. Our newsletter goes out to more than 5000 readers, writers, editors and publishers. The Web site is accessed over six million times each month.

ERWA has been favorably reviewed by *Playboy, Elle Magazine, AVN* online magazine, *Writer's Digest*, and recommended in a host of books and articles as the premier resource for erotica readers and writers. Every month, we entertain, educate and inform millions people from all over the globe who are interested in erotica.

Although we've grown tremendously, ERWA's strength is still in community. We are diverse and far-flung, but tightly connected. The result is an ongoing effort to understand and accept all persuasions, lifestyles, and expressions of sexuality. We want to bring the very best of erotica to readers, partly by helping writers excel in a genre that is making headlines and causing the entire publishing industry to sit up and take notice.

Personally, I'm amazed at what we've built together, and extremely proud. Now I can say to those frustrated folk who are searching, like I was, for sex writing that is simultaneously intelligent and arousing: here we are. Search no further. Welcome to ERWA. You're home.

– Adrienne Benedicks

CHAPTER 1: THE TEN COMMANDMENTS OF WRITING EROTICA

I. Thou Shalt Not Take the Lord's Name in Vain

"Ohgodohgodohgodohgodohgodohgodohgodohgodohgod." Need I say more? The same goes for any other kind of onomatopoeia: "ooh," "urg," "gack," "mmmm," etc. Use your words, people; *use your words!*

II. Thou Shalt Not Own a Thesaurus

This is an exaggeration, of course (to get that vicious Roget off my case). The need to change a descriptive word after every sentence or paragraph is the clear sign of an amateur. Example: "cock" in the first paragraph of the sex scene becomes "rod" in the second, "staff' in the third, "pole" in the forth ... and you get my gist. The same goes for the silly need to be *polite* in describing either a sex scene or various body parts. Unless you're writing a Victorian homage (or pastiche), women don't have a sex between their legs, and a member doesn't live in a man's trousers. If you can't write penis, clit, cock, cunt, or the rest of the words you can't say on television then find another job—or just write for television.

III. Thou Shalt Not Equate Dirty Movies with Erotic Writing

Films are films and stories are stories and very rarely do they meet. Another hallmark of the greenhorn is thinking that a erotic story has to have the deep characterization and suburban plotting of a porno film. Even a story written for the lowest of markets has to have something aside from sex scenes. So face it, just sitting down and writing out *Debbie Does Everyone* won't do anything but bore you and the reader.

IV: Thou Shalt Not Exaggerate (too much)

I'm big, but not the biggest—my girlfriend's tits are nice, but not the nicest in the world. Same should go for your stories. Unless you're being silly, keep your proportions to a human level. Every cock can't be tremendous; every pair of tits can't be the most beautiful, every cunt or asshole the tightest, etc. It's okay to hedge a bit, frame it with "- right then, at that moment -" or some such, but keep in mind that it's a cheap-shot at both sex and your readers to assume that desire can only be the result of seeing or fucking something of inhuman proportions: it only makes you look like the biggest of amateurs.

V: Thou Shalt Not Be Ignorant of Sex

Okay, it's perfectly reasonable not to be too realistic in describing sex—after all, erotic stories are supposed to be entertaining—but pointing out every nasty smell, or ... 'shortcoming' will make the reader anything but turned on. But there's still no excuse for making anatomical errors or perpetuating sexual myths. For example: simultaneous orgasms, "sucking" orgasms ("My g-spot is in my throat'), masochists who are automatically subservient, gay men who are attracted to every male who walks by, every woman is a potential bisexual, etc. I recommend research and empathy, trying to understand, exploring what sex is and what it isn't. Virgins (and the ignorant) after all can certainly write porno—they just can't write *good* porno.

VI: Thou Shalt Not Be Too Clever

I loved *Fight Club, The Sixth Sense,* and *The Usual Suspects*—but they worked because the screenwriters brilliantly knew how to tell an unusual story. It's another common myth that a story needs something mind-blowing to be entertaining—so many newbie writers will often try to toss in so many devices and situations because they're scared of boring the reader. As in all things, KISS: Keep It Simple, Stupid. Don't try to be too elaborate or devious—half the time the reader can see it coming a mile away. Rather than elaborate plotting or grandiose story constructions, concentrate instead on characterization, description, dialogue, a sense of place, pathos, wit, and *then* plot. Simplicity and subtlety can be dynamite, shock and surprise are just firecrackers—they don't move anything, and are often just annoying.

VII: Thou Shalt Not Write Porn

Unless, of course, that's what you're trying to write. I shall explain: too often editors get erotica that reads like something you'd buy in the bus station. Now if you're trying to write erection-producing materials suitable for long-distance public transportation then go for it. But if you're sending something off to, say, a "respectable" editor or publisher you should at least have a slight clue about what's being written and published for that market. A good technique is to throw out the idea what you're writing something that's supposed to get someone hard/wet: just tell a good damned story about sex. Just a long, drawn out sex scene with bad writing, no characters, no plot, atrocious dialogue, etc., isn't a story—even if you start with a title and conclude with THE END.

VIII: Thou Shalt Not Do Everything

Just because humans have cocks, cunts, clits, assholes, tits, nipples, mouths, noses, and hands doesn't mean you have to put them all, in their many and varied sexual interactions, in each and every story. After all, unless you have a free weekend and a Viagra IV drip, there's no way you could do it all—so how can you expect your characters in your story to? Simplicity again: sometimes a story screams for a blow and fuck, and sometimes all it needs is a long, lingering kiss. The story will often speak for itself—don't bow to the pressure of "I've done A, B, C, and D, so all I need to do to finish it off with E, F, G, and the rest of the alphabet." Good erotica is sweet, simple, and hot—bad erotica is clumsy, forced, and obvious.

IX: Thou Shalt Not Be Sterile

I don't mean well-scrubbed or squeaky clean; I mean that sex can be emotionally complex, that it can bring up a wide range of emotional states in the course of one romp in the hay: joy, happiness, ambivalence, exhaustion, anger, fear, disgust, guilt, etc. A story that's just about the sex, where everyone is happy, healthy, and horny is dull—the characters don't change, and nothing is revealed or explored. A story like that can lead to only one kind of emotion in the reader: boredom. Be daring, be risky, be dirty with your character's emotions. Use what you know, what you've been through, not just what you want to have happen. Life is icky, tricky, and messy—and what's what makes it great. Use it!

X: Thou Shalt Not Forget the Writing

It's easy enough. The pieces of a good story: plot, characterization, description, motivation, and all the rest of it, are so in the forefront of our minds that the fundamentals slip through the cracks. Now, I'm not talking about the real basics of spelling, grammar, and punctuation, but rather the real key of any story, erotica or not: the writing. After all, when you write a erotic story, you're writing a story first, and that it happens to be about sex is secondary. Plot, characterization, description, and motivation can add up to nothing if the writing itself is stilted, flat, or clunky. Writing should flow, sparkle, crackle, and evoke. It's a tough act, but really the most important. Don't let those obvious pieces get in the way of what you're doing: you're a writer, and telling a story.

* * * *

The bad news is that you can follow all of these Commandments and still fail if the writing isn't good, but the good news is that if you can do it—if you can amaze, amuse, or arouse with your words—then you can break any rule.

11

CHAPTER 2: DEFINITIVE DEFINITIONS

A pal of mine asked an interesting question once: what's my definition of erotica, or of pornography? Other folks have been asked these questions, of course, and the answers have been as varied as those asked, but even as I zapped off my own response I started to really think about how people define what they write, and more importantly, why.

It's easy to agree with folks who say there's a difference between erotica and pornography. One of the most frequent definitions is that erotica is sexually explicit literature that talks about something else aside from sex, while porno is sex, sex and more sex and nothing else. The problem with trying to define erotica is that it's purely subjective—even using the erotica-is-more-than-just-sex and porn-is-just-sex-analysis. Where's the line and when do you cross it? One person's literate erotica is another's pure filth. Others like to use a proportional scale a certain percent of sex content—bing!—something becomes porn. Once again: Who sets the scale?

What I find interesting isn't necessarily what the distinction between erotica and pornography should be but why there should be one to begin with. Some writers I've encountered seem to be looking for a clear-cut definition just so they won't be grouped together with the likes of *Hustler* and *Spank Me, Daddy*. While I agree that there's a big difference between what's being published in some of the more interesting anthologies, magazines and Web sites as opposed to *Hustler* and *Spank Me, Daddy*, I also think that a lot of this searching for a definition is more about ego and less about literary analysis. Rather than risk being put on the shelves next to *Hustler* and *Spank Me Daddy*, some writers try to draw up lists and rules that naturally favor what they write compared to what other people write: "I write erotica, but that other stuff is just pornography. Therefore what I write is better."

This thought process has always baffled me. First of all, it's completely subjective. Who died and made you arbiter of what's erotica and what's pornography? It sounds like those drawing the line have something to prove to themselves, or hide from. They decide it's okay to hate pornography because what I write is erotica. More importantly, this little fit of insecurity opens the door for other people to start using your own definitions against you. Even a casual glance at the politics of groups out to "save" us all from the evils of pornography shows that they will use any device, any subjective rule (otherwise known as "community

12

standards"), any nasty tactic to arrest, impound, burn, or otherwise erase what they consider to be dirty words. You might consider yourself an erotica writer, and be able to show certain people that you are—or, more importantly, convince yourself that you are—but to someone else you're nothing but a pornographer, just like the stories and writers from whom you're trying to distance yourself.

So I don't I'll tell you that personally, I use all the terms pretty much interchangeably: Porn, erotica, smut, literotica, and so forth. You name it, I use it. Depends on who's asking. If I'm writing to an editor or publisher, I use erotica. If I'm talking to another author, I playfully call myself a "smut" writer. If a Jesus Freak gets me out of bed with a knock on the door, I'm a damned pornographer. In my heart, though, I just call myself a writer because even though I write stories of butt-fucking bikers, lascivious cheerleaders, horny space aliens, and leathermen, I'm more turned on by trying to write an interesting story than what the story may particularly be about. Half the time I'm not even aware that what I'm writing is a sex story because I'm having way too much fun with alliteration, character, description, and plot! The fact that what I'm writing may appear in an anthology or book with the word "erotic" in the title has nothing to do with how I approach my writing: a story is a story no matter the amount or manner of the eroticism I may include. A good example of my commitment to writing, pure and simple, is that I sign my work M. Christian, no matter what I'm working on: science fiction, mystery, literary fiction, non-fiction, or even something with "erotic" in the title.

If there's a point to all this, it's that you're in charge of your own definitions, but try and pay attention to why you define, or why you feel you should. Erotica, pornography, smut, dirty words—be proud of what you write but never ever forget that genres, labels, brands, and all the rest are meaningless. If you're a writer, you write. And you get to call the fruits of your labor whatever you want because you created it.

CHAPTER 3: LEARNING THE ROPES

The inclination is natural, I suppose: we go to school to learn just about anything else, so why shouldn't there be a class or book or seminar that will teach you how to be a better smut writer?

Without getting too heady, the idea that there's a special — perhaps secret — way of getting you from bad to good, or unpublished to published, or unpaid to paid, is a bit disturbing. Ruminating a bit too much on it can make it all a bit like a paranoid fantasy, like there's a trick or a jealously guarded connection that allows other people to make it and keeps you out. But take my class, buy my book, attend my seminar and you too can learn the secret to successful erotica writing … just don't tell anyone.

Without gnawing off the hand that feeds me, I feel guilty teaching writing classes. Standing in front of a room full … well, a few dozen, tops … of green writers, all of them eagerly waiting for the secret makes me want to confess it all for a sham, and in so doing spill my guts on the real true way to become a better writer, of erotica or anything else.

Not that a class or two can't help, especially any classes that highlight some of the less-than-fun elements of a writer's life. If you're lucky, you might find the right kind of class, book, or seminar that gives — quickly and honestly — the sad facts of finding a market, writing a cover letter, formatting a story, dealing with publishers and editors, and so forth. Those kinds of books and classes can definitely help with the paperwork side of writing, especially since screwing any of it up can stop your story from even being read, much less considered. But they can't make you a better writer.

The worst of these kinds of classes and books are what I call Frog Killers. You've probably heard the analogy before: you can study how a frog is put together by taking it apart, but you can't put it together again afterwards. A book or class that focuses on picking apart a story — usually to a ridiculous set of specifications and standards — usually does nothing for new writers but make them hideously self-conscious. They write but then freeze up, panicking that they've forgotten the character transformation, that the story isn't emotionally engaging, that there's no conflict (man vs. man, man vs. nature, and whatever that other one is), that there's no clear A-B-C structure, and so forth. With this oppressive laundry list in their heads, yelling at them louder than their nascent creativity, no wonder budding writers can feel like deer caught in headlights. This is why, when someone's resume indicates that they have a degree in creative writing, I look at them like they'd stormed a hill under heavy enemy fire. It doesn't make them better writers, though, even though they might be able to tell you — to ten decimal places — why their story is worth publishing.

The other kind of book and class you might stumble across in your search for guidance is the philosophical one. To be honest, I like these much more than the Frog Killers — more than partially because it mirrors my own idea that writing is more magic than science. These kinds of teachers approach writing as art, usually with a series of literary touchy feely exercises that will stretch and tone your currently saggy imagination. The only problem with these is that they can all too often retreat from the idea of writing as being work, taking away the 90% perspiration in exchange for the 10% inspiration. Creativity is one thing, but you still have to get the damned thing down on paper.

As far as I know, the only way to be a better writer is ... drum roll, please ... to write. Not much of a surprise, is it? Some classes and books might be good for the basics, and for the nuts and bolts of the business. Forums might be fun; newsgroups might be a diversion, but the only thing that will make you a better writer is to do it, and not stop doing it.

It's a nasty rule, but aside from a few very rare exceptions, your first story will suck. It will suck painfully, forcefully, and with great vigor. So will your next one, and your next one, but eventually you'll get better: your language will begin to flow, and you won't be thinking about writing but will instead be telling a story. After that, you'll find yourself enjoying the process, nodding at little turns of phrase or a well-toned paragraph. Later you'll feel tears on your cheeks when you put THE END on something that worked out perfectly, beautifully.

Do you get where I'm going? No one can really teach you that, just like a paint-by-numbers kit won't turn you into Picasso. The only way you can really get better as a writer is to try and fail, try and fail, try and fail, try and fail, try and fail, try and fail, try and fail, try and get a bit better, try and get a bit better, try and do something good, try and good something better, try and make something great ....

So what are you reading this for? Get back to writing.

15

CHAPTER 4: LIVING THE LIFE

"The assassin readied himself, beginning first by picking up his trusty revolver and carefully threading a silencer onto the barrel."

That reads right enough, doesn't it? You look at it and it sings true. But it's not. Not because the assassin is a product of my imagination but because, except for one very rare instance, silencers cannot be fitted onto revolvers. So every time you see Mannix or Barnaby Jones facing off against some crook with a little tube on the end of their revolver, keep in mind that it has no bearing on reality.

What does this have to go with smut writing? Well, sometimes erotica writers—both old hands and new blood—make the same kind of mistakes: not so much a revolver with a silencer, but definitely the anatomical or psychological equivalent.

People ask me sometimes what kind of research I do to write erotica. The broad answer is that I seriously don't do that much true research, but I do observe and try and understand human behavior—no matter the interest or orientation—and add that to what I write. But that doesn't mean that there isn't some (ahem) fieldwork involved.

I'm very lucky to have started writing erotica here in San Francisco. If America has a sexual organ, it's here. Good example: do you know what the most-attended parade is in the US? Answer: The Rose Parade in Pasadena. No surprise there, right? Well, here's one: do you know the second most-attended parade? It's the San Francisco Lesbian/Gay/Bisexual/Trans-gendered Day Parade. There are 500,000 people—some gay and some not, all cheering for love and sex. It's more than mind-blowing; it's truly inspiring. It also shows how sexy this burg is. I should also mention the Folsom Street Fair: 400,000 leather- and latex-clad men, women, and genderqueers thronging through seven blocks of the city.

Sex is not just in the atmosphere here; it's also a tradition. The Institute for the Study of Human Sexuality is here, and SFSI is here. SFSI stands for San Francisco Sex Information, a completely self-funded sex information and referral system. It works like this: after 52 hours of training (doctors get only something like 15), volunteers are qualified to go on the switchboard and answer questions from all over the country on any aspect of human sexuality without judgment, bias, or giggles. If you call (415) 989-7374 one of these volunteers will answer whatever you ask, or put you in contact with another group who will. It's a wonderful service and an invaluable resource. You can also check them out at www.sfsi.org.

It's easy to make the assumption that you're well informed, but the fact is we are being bombarded by prejudice and simply inaccurate information all the time. The media is getting better at depicting sexuality, but they still have a long way to go. Way too often I'll read a book, watch a movie, or flip channels, and groan at some cliché being perpetuated: all gay men are effeminate, all lesbians are butch, S/M is destructive, polyamorous people are sex-addicted, older people don't have sex, couples always orgasm together—the list goes on and on. Many of these things are done out of laziness—but others are repetition of what the creators honestly believe are true.

It's a very hard to unlearn something you've always taken as truth, and even harder to recognize what's in your personal worldview that needs to be reexamined. My advice is to assume, especially in regards to sexuality, that everything you know should be looked at again. If you're right, then the worst you can do is perhaps add a bit more to your knowledge, or get a different perspective. But if you crack open a book, or blip to a Web site, and find yourself going "I didn't know that," then feel good rather than bad: by doing that, and adding it to your erotic fiction, you'll help perpetuate accuracy rather than bullcrap.

One more thing you could do is help people. We don't like sex in this country. Sure, we sell beer and cars with it, but we don't like it. We're scared of it. Living in this world with anything that's not beer and car commercial sexuality can be a very frightening and lonely experience. Too many people feel that they are alone, or what they like to do sexually is wrong, sinful, or sick. Now I'm not talking about violent or abusive sexual feelings, but rather an interest in something that harms no one and that other people have discovered to be harmless or even beneficial. If you treat what you're writing about with respect, care, and understanding, you could reach out to someone, somewhere and help them understand and maybe even get through their bad feelings about their sexuality—bad feelings, by the way, that more than likely have been dished out by the lazy and ignorant for way too long.

In other words, especially in regards to erotica, you should be part of the solution and not the problem.

ASK A PROVOCATEUR: LISABET SARAI

What makes a great erotic story?

Palpable desire that goes beyond mere physical arousal. In a great erotic story, the reader will identify with the characters and experience intense longing for the object of his/her affections. The sort of desire I'm talking about can take many forms, but its signature is the fact that it feels irresistible and overwhelming. It trumps considerations of propriety, convenience, even morality.

Obviously a *great* erotic story also needs an original premise, intriguing yet believable characters, expressive language and all the other characteristics of great stories in general. It is the experience of desire, however, that sets erotic stories apart.

* * * *

What would you tell someone who is just starting out as an erotica writer?

Write your passion. Begin by creating stories that push your own buttons and explore your own fantasies. As a writer develops, she may need to expand her range of subject matter and disguise her personal kinks, but I still believe that the best erotica is fueled by the author's own libido.

* * * *

What's a common mistake writers make when writing erotica?

Focusing too much on the physical aspects of sex. In my view, sex without emotion is empty and boring. The sexual activities in an erotic story (if any!) should flow from the characters' needs, desires and fantasies, and the sex scenes should remain centered in the characters' heads as they think, feel and react to what's happening to their bodies.

* * * *

Lisabet Sarai has been writing and publishing erotica since 1999 and has five novels, two short story collections, and two erotica anthologies to her credit. Her stories have appeared in more than two dozen collections including the past four years' Mammoth Book Of Best New Erotica. Recently she began ePublishing with Total-E-Bound, Eternal Press and Phaze. Lisabet also reviews erotica for the Erotica Readers and Writers Association and Erotica Revealed.

CHAPTER 5: WHO ARE YOU?

Writers are professional liars: it's our job is to tell a story so well that the audience believes it's the truth, at least for the course of the story. The technical term, of course, is *suspension of disbelief*—the trick of getting the reader to put aside any doubts that what you're saying isn't the truth, the whole truth, so help you God.

For erotica writers, that means convincing the reader that you really are a college cheerleader named Tiffany who likes stuffed animals and gang-bangs with the football team ... or that you're a pro tennis player named Andre who has a mean backhand and can suck cock like a professional. A writer's job is to convince, to put aside doubts ... in other words, to lie through their fucking teeth.

As any liar worth their salt knows, the trick to telling a good one is to mix just the right amount of truth with the bullshit. You don't tell your mom you went to the movies rather than church; you say you had a sick friend, that your car broke down or that you had a cold. The same goes for fiction: spinning something that everyone knows is a lie ("the check is in the mail") is flimsy, but adding the right amount of real life experience makes a story really *live*. Rather than Tiffany and the football players, how about a young woman who really wants to do a gangbang, but doesn't know how to break it to her boyfriend or girlfriend? We've all had the experience of trying to find a way to communicate our sexual fantasies to someone, so that rings true ... even though our character is a total fabrication.

The same goes for dialogue, both external and internal. One of the worst cases I've seen came from, believe it or not, a mainstream book, where one character actually thought: *I am happy with my homosexuality*—and the intent was not humor or sarcasm. Orientation, like a lot of things in our lives, is something that's just *there*, an integral part of our mental landscape: so integral that we don't need to express it to ourselves as a thought.

While I do say that writing is lying, I don't want you to extend that to professional identity. What I mean is that while it's okay to *be* someone for a story, that falsehood should end with you who are as a person. Let's say you've written a kick-ass gay men's erotic story, and you're a woman; don't send the story with a cover letter saying that your name is Stanley and you live in San Francisco with your life partner, Paul.

Do you get where I'm going? You can say what you want in your fiction, but when you cross that line to try and lie to the editor or publisher you're not telling a story, you're being deceptive. Now there's no rule about using all kinds of different pseudonyms (I have three, myself) but I'm also clear about who I am, and what I am, to an editor or publisher. There's no reason to announce everything about yourself in a cover letter, but there's a big difference between not saying something and trying to trick an editor.

There's recently been a minor spate of this happening: men and women trying to be something they are not, for whatever reasons. Like I said, fiction is one thing, but anything beyond fiction is ... well, weird at least, and stupid at worst. The fact is that we writers and editors all talk to each other, and eventually the truth will come out. It might not be a criminal offense, but I don't mind being tricked by a story—but never in the real world of business dealings.

In short, it's much better to be open and honest in a professional capacity, and leave the sex and lies for your stories where they belong.

CHAPTER 6: RISKS

"The shock of September 11 is subsiding. Each day adds distance. Distance diminishes fear. Cautiously our lives are returning to normal. But "normal" will never be the same again. We have seen the enemy and the enemy is among us .... the publishers, producers, peddlers and purveyors of pornography."

It didn't take me long to find that quote. It came from an LDS Web site, Meridian Magazine, but I could have picked fifty others. In light of that kind of hatred, I think it's time to have a chat about what it can mean to ... well, do what we do.

We write pornography. Say it with me: por-nog-ra-phy. Not erotica—a word too many writers use to distance themselves, or even elevate themselves, from the down and dirty stuff on most adult bookstore shelves—but smut, filth ... and so forth.

I've mentioned before how it's dangerous to draw a line in the sand, putting fellow writers on the side of smut and others in erotica. The Supreme Court couldn't decide where to scrawl that mark—what chance do we have?

What good are our petty semantics when too many people would love to see us out of business or thrown in jail? They don't see any difference between what I write and what you write. We can sit and argue all we like over who's innocent and who's guilty until our last meals arrive, but we'll still hang together.

I think it's time to face some serious facts. Hyperbole aside, we face some serious risks for putting pen to paper or file to disk. I know far too many people who have been fired, stalked, threatened, had their writing used against them in divorces and child custody cases, and much worse.

People hate us. Not everyone, certainly, but even in oases like San Francisco, people who write about sex can suffer tremendous difficulties. Even the most—supposedly—tolerant companies have a hard time with an employee who writes erotica. A liberal court will still look down on a defendant who has published stories in *Naughty Nurses*. The religious fanatic will most certainly throw the first, second, third stone—or as many as it takes—at a filth peddler.

This is what we have to accept. Sure, things are better than they have been before and, if we're lucky, they will slowly progress, but we all have to open our eyes to the ugly truths that can accompany a decision to write pornography.

What can we do? Well, aside from calling the ACLU, there isn't a lot to we can directly do to protect ourselves if the law, or Bible-wielding fanatics, break down our doors — but there are a few relatively simple techniques you can employ to be safe. Take these as you will, and keep in mind that I'm not an expert in the law, but never forget that what you're doing can be dangerous.

Assess your risks. If you have kids, have a sensitive job, own a house, have touchy parents, or live in a conservative city or state, you should be extra careful about your identity. Even if you think you have nothing to lose, you do — your freedom. Many cities and states have very loose pornography laws, and all it would take is a cop, a sheriff, or a district attorney to decide you needed to be behind bars to put you there.

Hide. Yes, I think we should all be proud of what we do, what we create, but use some common sense about how easily you can be identified or found: use a pseudonym and a post office box, never post your picture, and so forth. Women, especially, should be extra careful. I know far too many female writers who have been stalked or Internet-attacked because of what they do.

Keep your yap shut. Don't tell your bank, your boss, your accountant, your plumber, or anyone at all, what you do. When someone asks, I say I'm a writer. If I know them better, I say I write all kinds of things — including erotica. If I know them very, very, very well, then maybe I'll show them my newest book. People (it shouldn't have to be said) are very weird. Just because you like someone doesn't mean you should divulge that you just sold a story to *Truckstop Transsexuals.*

Support our allies. Remember that line we drew between pornography and erotica? Well, here's another: you might be straight, you might be bi, but in the eyes of those who despise pornography you are just as damned and perverted as a filthy sodomite. It makes me furious to meet a homophobic pornographer. Every strike against gay rights is another blow to your civil liberties and is a step closer to you being censored, out of a job, out of your house, or in jail. You can argue this all you want, but I've yet to see a hysterical homophobe who isn't anti-erotica. For you to be anti-gay isn't just an idiotic prejudice, it's giving the forces of puritanical righteousness even more ammunition for their war.

I could go on, but I think I've given you enough to chew on. I believe that writing about sex is something that no one should be ashamed of, but I also think that we all need to recognize and accept that there are many out there who do not share those feelings. Write what you want, say what you believe, but do it with your eyes open. Understand the risks, accept the risks and be smart about what you do — so you can keep working and growing as a writer for many years to come.

CHAPTER 7: OCCUPATIONAL HAZARD

Other writers get it, of course: romance writers live in rosy castles and have crinoline dreams; science fiction authors are pasty-faced nerds with more love for science than humanity; horror pros keep corpses in their basement for research.

It's natural for people to think that because you write erotica ... well, it's pretty obvious that they think: thin, greasy mustaches, seedy domains, hacks, perverts — the clichés pop immediately to mind. But what's really interesting is that this isn't the toughest of occupational hazards for the erotica writer. After all, life is full of surprises: the romance author is a cynical young guy, the science fiction writer can't balance her checkbook, the horror fan loves Fred Astaire movies, and the erotica writer is just doing a job.

Who cares what other people think: it's what's inside you that counts — and what's inside erotica can be very unusual, sometimes almost traumatic.

The romance writer might fall in love with one of his or her characters, science fiction writers might be endlessly frustrated that they're living in the past and not the future they love, and horror writers might look at the world through a serial killer's eyes, but smut writers deal with very loaded stuff every time they pick up their metaphorical pens. Sex is powerful: it lives in the deepest parts of us, lurking in the brainstem right up there with climbing in the trees. It's also very unpredictable. Sex isn't intellectual; changing our sexual selves is like trying to change left or right-handedness. Despite what hysterical fundamentalists believe, sexual orientation isn't something that can be cured — don't even bother to try. In short, sex is the atomic bomb of the psyche.

When you write erotica, you have to be prepared to be surprised. When anyone sits down to write fiction, they casually flip through their lives, loves, and experience to fill in the blanks. This character is white, this character is black, this character is straight, gay, tall, short, fat, thin, nasty, sweet ... this character is (fill in the blank). When you write stories with a sexual focus, those choices can sometimes reveal deep sexual feelings — feelings that can emerge in unexpected ways.

One of the big decisions erotica writers have to face is a professional one: write what you like and what you know, or try to write about other orientations or practices. Stick to familiar territory and your market is very limited—but even if you stick to your own sexual neighborhood, you still can be in for some surprises. Write the same kind of story, even if it's as broad as your orientation with no queer or S/M overtones, enough times and something is bound to emerge. Maybe it's the location, the description of the characters, the sex act itself—something is going to pop up. A memory will emerge, a revelation of a certain sexual peculiarity will dawn on you—and you'll find yourself staring at a blank page, shivering.

I've known writers who've found themselves unexpectedly aroused by a story that's taken a dark, even horrifyingly sexual turn—or straight writers getting turned on by writing gay porno, and vice versa. I've had the experience myself, getting honestly disturbed by a story I'd been writing. While I definitely encourage writers to try new and unique approaches to writing, I also warn them about these surprises—they're part of the game for being an erotica writer.

What to do about it? Like anything psychological, there isn't a cure-all technique. But why should you try and cure it? It's part of you. Maybe it's something small, maybe something indicative of a larger issue, but it's still part of who you are. Personally, I try to really look at what pops up, and how it makes me feel. Is it frightening, the emotions that came up during the writing of that one story, or is it a theme that I hadn't been aware of? An editor of mine pointed out that a lot of my stories take place at dusk or dawn, between day and night. When I heard this, I was shocked and angry that I'd subconsciously used the same device over and over again, but then I realized that for me it was also a way of using a curtain between our walking-around selves and our sexual selves. Another friend of mine recently realized that most of his characters have a certain color hair and eyes. Not the end of the world, certainly, but still exposing something laying deep in the mind.

When the discoveries are more shocking, one thing I try and remember is what I call the horror hazard. Horror writers have the same visceral reaction to their work: thinking too much about how much blood a decapitation would generate, or the sound a hatchet would make cutting off a limb. It doesn't mean they want to try it, but the images are too real … too vivid. Writers, remember, use their imaginations, and imaginations are made of jumbled experience and rearranged thoughts. It doesn't mean that the wish is father to the action, it just means that you've managed to impress your own consciousness with your skill as a storyteller. You've surprised your own mind.

Good or bad, it is simply an unusual discovery or an indication of something deeper, something disturbing, and these things happen. Whether you decide to let it bother you, use it for self-exploration, or smile at the fact that your writing managed to arouse yourself is up to you. The best advice I can give is to remember two little things when it does happen: like anything to do with sex, you are not alone. We all have had our similar moments, the same fears and disturbing thoughts. The other is that you're a writer, remember: a teller of stories, a professional liar. Your life, your dreams, your thoughts are fodder for your work, and that sometimes using the stuff that might scare you or make you uncomfortable is the best thing. In other words, when things are uncomfortable, try exploring further: write it out and see where it goes.

That's an occupational hazard, but it can also be the greatest reward.

CHAPTER 8: THE HARD PART

Thinking of a story isn't usually the hard part. Sometimes the plot doesn't work, or it's too much like everything else I've ever read or seen on the big or small screen.

But other times it just works. On those occasions, I can see the story and visualize it as a series of scenes. Parts of it are so clear they feel as though they were written right in the forefront of my mind. I know it's going to be good. That's wondrous.

Writing the story can be challenging, but it's not really hard. There are times when it's not what I've seen in my head, and it just falls apart: the words fail, the descriptions are tired, the great plot in my mind turns to crap on the page ... but then occasionally something else pops up, and something that was almost too small to notice in the original story flares up into a brilliance (if I do say so myself).

Don't ask me the secret, because I don't know it. Not everything I write is great and not everything is garbage. If there is a literary legerdemain, it might be that you just have to write ten pieces of crud to produce one priceless jewel. That's a lot of crud, but when you hold that jewel in your hand and know that you made it, the feeling is indescribable. That's why it's possible to keep writing, even when so many of the stories turn out to be awful: you know that if you keep working, one of them could be the special one. But that's not the hard part.

Polishing and re-writing can be a bitch, but that's not the hard part either. Sometimes it's quick and easy: my copy editor can't find any mistakes, my spell checker breezes through the thing without a beep or a hiccup, or maybe something better pops into my mind for a scene. Then there are times when I kick the tires and the engine falls out: I show it to a pal and that wonderful plot device bores him stiff. Beautiful writing suddenly reads clunky and overblown or just flat and lifeless. Sometimes I read it again and realize that what I thought was a jewel is a mud pie. But that's not the hard part, because I can put the story in a drawer and forget about it, or try again.

Finding a place to send a story can be hard, but it's not the most trying part of the job. There are times I work to spec: a call for submissions flashes across my attention, and—bang—the story gets written and sent out. Other times I work *just because I want to*. These are often great stories, but selling them can be a stone cold bitch. Maybe there's not enough sex, or maybe there's too much; maybe there's too much fantasy/science fiction/horror, or most often, not enough. So the story gets stuck in a drawer somewhere, and next time when one of those calls for submissions comes out, the story goes. Sometimes, they never find a home. Orphaned and unwanted, they sit in my various machines and gather digital dust. That's sad, but it's not terribly painful, because occasionally I take them out of their electronic sleep and fall in love with them all over again. Knowing they are there, and that I wrote them, somehow makes it all okay.

As for finding those places, I have a network of spies and friends who zap them to me, and I spend slow afternoons crawling the web. I look over publications that I think I might like to write a story for, or I might have a stored masterpiece that could work for them.

The hardest part happens after all the preceding come out just right: the idea gels, the writing flows, a perfect market opens up ... and then the rejection slip arrives. I say this often, and I really feel it's true: writing isn't for wimps. Unlike a lot of other hobbies or careers, writing is just you and your imagination alone in a little room. When that rejection slip comes you can't blame the back-up band, the guy who didn't deliver the package overnight, or even God. When that rejection slip comes it's your work, your imagination, on trial.

There is a commandment I try to follow: celebrate the story, not the sale. Relish the writing, and enjoy getting it right on the page. Focusing too much on publishing puts your happiness in someone else's hands. I try to put myself in the editor's place, but even when I recall some of my own decisions as an editor, and when I remind myself how completely subjective those acceptances can be, there's still that sting. They didn't like my story. I failed.

Sniffle.

There is a better solution. It really works, and it's not even all that complex. You will still feel pain when the rejection comes, but if you do this little procedure I can pretty much guarantee the pain will fade.

Keep On Working. Dab your eyes and start again. Think of a story, write it down, try to find a place to send it ... lather, rinse, repeat. Do this enough times and I can all but promise that one day you'll get a contract rather than a rejection. Work, and try to advance: not in paycheck or status, but in the delight you take in writing. Your stories might sit in drawers, they might take up hard drive space, and they might bounce time and time again from one publication to the next, but if you feel good about yourself and your work, then it'll all get easier and better.

If all you care about is the sale, your writing career will be nothing but a series of rejections broken by the occasional sale. If you stop, breathe, and enjoy the art of writing, then the only hard part will be finding enough time to tell your wonderful stories.

27

ASK A PROVOCATEUR: DONNA GEORGE STOREY

What makes a great erotic story?

A great erotic story has all the components of a great literary or mystery story: complex characters, a compelling conflict, well-crafted prose, vivid detail and a multi-layered richness of imagery and meaning so that you definitely get more out of a second reading than the first.

But there's also that *erotic* part of the equation. Eroticism is such an important force in the human experience and yet throughout most of history, and in many respects even today, honest expression about this topic has been repressed. So a great erotic story for me always pushes the boundaries to speak the truth about sex and love and desire. What makes power play so alluring? How does swinging enrich a couple's relationship? What new things can you see through a blindfold? Great erotica gives us the chance to break free from our society's fear of sex to illuminate the mysteries of the sexual urge.

* * * *

What would you tell someone who is just starting out as an erotica writer?

There are no original plots or characters. What each writer contributes to the cause of erotica—which I define as sex between two complex human beings rather than two mechanical bodies—is her or his sensibility. So you'll tell ancient stories, but you'll tell them in the way only you can do.

The writing life is not kind to the ego, but love for your work will carry you through. Write about what fascinates you, scares you, turns you on fiercely. Readers can feel your passion, just as they can tell when you're filling in the blanks in a formula. There are so many fringe benefits to giving yourself to your stories heart, mind and body. As a writer, it is your pleasurable duty to pay close attention to the world around you, to the taste and texture of your lover's skin, the smell of his sweat, the way his fingers curve when they cup your breast. Appreciating and capturing these sensual details is your *work*. And sure, the money's not great, but I've never had a better job!

* * * *

What's a common mistake writers make when writing erotica?

Worrying other people will think you're a pervert. Whether you use a pseudonym or not, I think every erotica writer encounters a moment—or several—when a little voice whispers "you can't write this filthy smut." But remember, the writer's calling to tell the truth is a noble one. Try

28

your best create a safe space for yourself when you're writing sex. No one is watching you: no parents or teachers or ministers. Not even God—She's on coffee break. Then when you're all alone, you can get wild!

And it's very likely the people you imagine are judging you have plenty of sick, dirty fantasies of their own.

The other mistake I see is the focus on getting published as validation for your writing. Sure, it's great to see your byline, but what really matters is the writing itself. If you write about things that fascinate you, if you write with passion, editors will eventually pick up on that and they'll publish you. The first erotic story I ever wrote was rejected over and over, but a few years later, when I'd published some other stories, Bill Noble picked it up for *Clean Sheets*. Then it was chosen for Maxim Jakubowski's *Mammoth Book of Best New Erotica*, and reprinted several more times. So patience and persistence do pay off!

* * * *

Donna George Storey's fiction has been published in over a hundred literary and erotica anthologies. She is author of Amorous Woman, *the steamy tale of an American woman's love affair with Japan. Read more of her work at www.DonnaGeorgeStorey.com.*

29

CHAPTER 9: USING THE RIGHT WORDS

Erotic writing isn't any different than any other form of writing: you still need a plot, characterization, description, a sense of place, suspension of disbelief, and so forth. Thinking otherwise will only put training wheels on your writing, which—believe me—readers and editors can easily pick up on. If you sit down and try to write a damned good story that happens to be about sex or sexuality, the result will generally be much finer artistically than an attempt that's just tossed off. The instant you approach a story as *just* anything, you'll demean yourself and the reader. The bottom line is that there really isn't much of a difference between a great erotic story and any other genre's great story.

One difference between erotica and other genres is that erotica doesn't blink: in just about every other genre, when sex steps on stage the POV swings to fireplaces, trains entering tunnels, and the like. In other words, it blinks away from the sexual scene. In erotica you don't blink, you don't avoid sexuality; you integrate it into the story. But the story you're telling isn't just the sex scene(s), it's why the sex IS the story. Something with a bad plot, poor characterization, lousy setting, or lazy writing and a good sex scene is always much worse than a damned good story full of interesting characters, a great sense of place, sparkling writing and a lousy sex scene. The sex scene(s) can be fixed, but if the rest—the meat of the story itself—doesn't work, you're only polishing the saddle on a dead horse.

Aside the lack of blinking, the other difference erotica and other genres is repetition: a lot of people preach that it's poor writing to use the same descriptive word too many times in the same section of writing. In other words:

The sun blasted across the desert, scorching scrub and weed into burnt yellow, turning soft skin to lizard flesh, and metal to rust. Outside LAST CHANCE FOR GAS, the radiation of the explosion had turned once gleaming signs for COCA-COLA and DIESEL into rust-pimpled ghosts of their former selves.

Parked outside LAST CHANCE, there was a rusted pickup collapsed onto four flat tires, the windshield a sparkling spider web under the hard white light of the sun's explosion.

That wasn't terrific, but the point is—aside from the poor metaphor of the sun as an explosion—the word *rust* springs up a bit too much. It's not *that* bad a description, but having the same word pop up repeatedly comes off as lazy, unimaginative, or simply dull. To keep this from happening, many writing teachers and guides recommend varying the descriptive vocabulary. Now you don't need to change rust to *corrosion* or *decay* or *encrustation* once you've used it once in a story, but if you need to use the same kind of description in the same paragraph or section, you might want to slip in some other, perhaps equally evocative, words as well.

But let's go onto that exception for erotica. In smut, we have a certain list of words that are required for a well-written erotic scene: the vocabulary of genitalia and sex. If you follow the *Don't Ever Repeat* rule in a sex scene, the results are often more hysterical than stimulating.

Bob's cock was so hard it was tenting his jeans. He desperately wanted to touch it, but didn't want to rush. Still, as he sat there, the world boiled down to him, what he was watching, and his penis. Finally, he couldn't take it anymore. Carefully, slowly, he lowered his zipper and carefully pulled his dick out. Unlike a lot of his friends, Bob was happy with his member. It was long, but not too long, and had a nice, fat head. Unlike the rods his friends rarely described, his pole didn't bend — but was nice and straight.

It's another bit of less-than-brilliance, but, hopefully, you'll get the idea: if you follow the non-repeat commandment, you'll quickly run out of words to describe what the hell's going on in your story. With women's anatomy it gets even worse: I've read a lot of amateur stories that go from *cunt* to *pussy* to *quim* to *hole* to *sex*, somehow turning a down-and-dirty contemporary piece to a story that should be called *Lady Rebecca and the Highwayman*.

It's more than perfectly okay to repeat certain words in a story — especially an erotic one — if other words just won't work, or will give the wrong impression (is there anything less sexy than using *hole* or *shaft*?). My advice is to stick to two or three words that fit the time and style of the story, then rotate them: cock to dick, pussy to cunt, etc. Some words can also be used if you feel the story is getting a bit too thin on descriptions — penis, crotch, groin, etc. — but only if kept to a very dull roar.

One of the best ways to avoid this problem is to describe parts of the character's anatomy rather than using a simple, general word. For example, lips, clit, glans, balls, shaft, mons, etc. Not only does this give you more flexibility, but it can also be wonderfully evocative, creating a complex image rather than a fuzzy impression of the party going on in your characters' pants.

The bottom line is what while there is a core similarity between a good erotic story and any other genre, there are a few important stylistic differences — and, as the old saying goes: *viva la difference!*

31

CHAPTER 10: DIRTY WORDS

Very few genres have their writers picking and choosing—often very carefully—what words they can, should, or must never use. In erotica, word choice basically comes down to two questions: what's appropriate to the story, and how important is it to work around limitations.

Believe it or not, certain editors and publishers have a *verboten* word list that includes certain slang terms or spellings. The question of whether to argue with them isn't an ethical one. Your preference for *cum* rather than *come* or your use of *pussy* when the editor doesn't favor it isn't really the question. Your main dilemma is simply this: how much you want to see your work published? Editors will insist you take it out or publishers will often change the word without your permission, so really, how attached are you to these words?

For the record, I believe an anthology should be consistent in its spelling—so while I respect a writer's preference for *come* instead of *cum* I don't blink, or blink that much, when my publisher suggests a change so the word is the same in every story. In the second instance, if an editor or publisher simply doesn't like a word ... well, I suggest the editor go into therapy, and that the rest of us simply try not to sweat it when they take the word out. And we can always just not work with them in the future.

Now appropriate word choice: that's another matter. Certain words either aren't correct or don't *feel* correct in the context of a story. The problem could be historical. For example, the word *sex* as a term for female genitalia is tolerable when you're doing a historical piece, but when your character is a Gen-X, Y, or Z person, how appropriate is it? It might be technically correct, but *sex* is often used as a safe way of describing what's between a woman's thighs. My own rule is to use terms that feel right for the character. If someone is depicted as repressed, using words like *cunt* or *twat* is jarring. Same for an older man using clumsy slang for his own genitals, like *member*.

I applaud people for doing research, by the way. Nothing adds a flavor of realism more than slipping in a good word choice for sex or the active biology of sex. One of my own favorites is a 19th century term for female genitalia, *Old Hat*, because it was *frequently felt*. Yes, you may wince.

One thing I like to see in a story has little to do with the words of sex and more to do with the view of sex. Assuming that characters in a story set in Nero's Rome view sex the same way we do today can result in some clumsy word usage. Certain types of sex were rare or seen with disfavor—in the case of Rome, noticing or even admiring women's breasts in a sexual context was a sign of weakness. Just look at the Pompeii mosaics; the prostitutes depicted—no matter what they were doing—kept their boobies wrapped. Therefore, you wouldn't want to spend too much time waxing poetic on some Roman woman's tits if your story was set in that time period.

The bottom line is that certain words and ideas work and others don't. The trick to picking the right ones has little to do with the power of them at this moment or your own personal preference as it does with their relevance within the story. Naughty words shouldn't be ones that reach the modern libido but instead be used to continue to keep the reader within and enjoying the story. Because when you get down to it, an erotic story isn't about the words but rather what you are saying with them.

CHAPTER 11: THE RIGHT AMOUNT

What *is* the right amount of sexy content for an erotic story? In other words how do you know what's not enough, too much, or just right?

The answer is actually pretty simple. But before that punch line, let's take a few minutes to think about the question. Erotic stories, by their nature, should have some level of sexually explicit material in them—the same way a Western has to be set in the west, fantasy has to have an air of unreality, mystery has to have a body somewhere, and so forth. But what makes a story erotic? Some people use a Peter Meter: if the story excites the reader then it succeeds as erotica. The problem with that is obvious: what gets my motor going isn't going to have an effect on someone else. One man's turn-on may very well be a woman's yawn. Besides, stories should be written with the mind, not the dick (or female equivalent). When they are created with the wrong set of organs, they come off about as legible as a bout of cybersex: "Oooooh baby yes stroke it for me."

So if excitement isn't the criterion, then what is? If you're writing for a particular market that has very specific needs, those requirements are definitely going to be a factor in the story's salability. Not that a work that doesn't comply with that market's standards is *bad*, it's just that those publishers simply won't buy something they know their readership won't like. Though the type and flavor (rough, romantic, subtle, surreal, etc.) of sex in an erotic story is a factor in meeting the needs of a particular market, very rarely does a market demand the amount of sexual content.

So if the market doesn't really dictate the amount of sex in a sex story, then what does? Some writers use a kind of mathematical rule, a percentage of length, kind of like one of those horrible test questions we've all had: "If Bobby the leatherman has a nine-inch dick and he's whipping Charley, a sub with six hard inches, then at what point will Bobby suck Charley and for how long?"

This requirement idea of erotica also comes up when writers think they have to include a certain amount or type of sexual activity in their stories. For my money, sex is too wide a field to be hemmed in by a checklist of activities: oral, intercourse, anal, S/M, orgasm, and so forth. In fact, the variations are too vast to cover every possible activity. With the enormity of such a task in mind, the most common default formula becomes the idea of at least one orgasm per story. But even this approach isn't absolute. Many writers manage to write very, very good stories with plenty of sensual, erotic content without any earthquakes or fireworks.

The idea of some kind of hard and firm (sorry) rule towards writing — erotica or anything else — is full of holes. Aside from cluttering up writers' desks with protractors and calculators, it turns art into a science and while I'm a huge supporter of the scientific method, I'd rather keep bubbling beakers, x-ray machines, statistical analysis, and gas chromatographs out of my office, my publishers' and editor's offices, as well as my bedroom.

So if there isn't a formulaic breakdown for erotica then how *do* you know when it's not too hot, not cool cold, but rather just right? Ready for the answer? Are you *sure* you're ready? Well here it is: *you just do.*

Writing is in no way a certain, quantifiable thing. It's an art, and like all art it comes through craft, discipline, self-examination, and a lot of trial and error. Similarly, it's unique and totally individual. My erotica won't read like his, hers, theirs, or anyone else's — and thank goodness for that. Sure, some publishers may promise their readers some laser-targeted smut, but they still don't want exactly the same story, over and over and over again.

The amount of sex I put into a story very often has to do with the story I'm trying to write, as determined by what I want the reader to get out of the experience. Sometimes it's a very small amount, because the story may simply call for it, while other times everyone is getting it on with everyone else with barely any room for anything, or anyone, else. In other cases, a story may be more about sex than actually showing physical sex, which means the whole story may be sexual but no one takes their clothes off or even has an orgasm.

Stories can be memories, reminiscences, or distracted fantasies; sex scenes can be pages or just a few choice paragraphs; body parts can be described in one word, or hundreds. The same goes for every other genre: science fiction doesn't always mean a lot of science; romance doesn't have to have a completely happy ending; horror can be funny as well as scary. Every writer is different, so every story is different — just as it should be.

So the answer — simple and direct — is that the right amount of sex for an erotic story is whatever is right for that one story, and the only way to find that line is to keep writing, keep trying. One day, if you keep working, you won't even think about it and the story itself will let you know what to show, and what to hide — and what will be exactly the right amount!

CHAPTER 12: BEING A REAL CHARACTER

Characters are the heart and soul of any fiction, erotic or otherwise. You can have a great plot, vivid descriptions, and nuances up the wazoo, but if your characters act like sock puppets—spouting endless clichés, doing stupid things for stupid reasons, and in general acting nothing like real people—the reader's disbelief is not suspended and the story doesn't work.

So how do you breathe life into a character? In my experience as an editor, I can tell you that stiffness instantly shows in a poorly written character. What is stiffness? Well, some of the best examples I can think of aren't in writing, but in movies or television. You've seen it: an actor or actress gives a bad performance, being stilled or monotone with no inflection. On the page, that shows up when a character thinks, does, or says something wooden, lifeless, or obviously forced to get the author's point across.

I'll let you in on a little secret. Do you know how to make a character live on the page? It's kind of scary, which is why I suppose a lot of writers don't do it, and it shows in their work. Are you ready? Are you really ready? Honestly? Okay, here goes: look inward, my child.

Thank ewe, thank ewe; just put some money in the basket on the way out. What, you want more? Sheesh! Okay, kidding aside, my favorite way of adding depth and ... well, call it *character* to a character is to get into yourself, your own emotional landscape, and your own history. Do you honestly look at someone and think: *I would like to have sex with him or her?* Nah, and if you do, I suggest immediate therapy. What really happens is much more primal and base. It's like your subconscious takes over and snaps your head around, or you find yourself absently daydreaming, imagining what sex with them would be like. Your imagination runs wild.

Let's say you're straight: you don't know what gay sex is like. Fine. But you *do* know what sex is like for you: the nervousness, the heady arousal, the way your mind races, your senses go rocketing, and so forth. The rest is just mechanics. The problem with this, and the main reason I feel why there are so many bad characters out there, is that it means exposing yourself on the page. Adding yourself (your feelings, emotions, and so forth) to a character is like a voodoo spell. Your fictional shade becomes connected to you. If the story gets rejected, it hits really hard. It's like a part of you being turned down.

Still, I think it's the way to go. But what if you're describing someone who doesn't share your experience? Let's say they are in mortal danger, or in jail, or unstable; how the hell do you make that character real? What I do is close my eyes and put on that person, and walk a while in his or her shoes. Are they frightened? You know what fear is like. Angry? You know what being pissed off is like. What draws their attention? What are they looking for and why? These are not just plot points here, but perspective: how the character relates to the world and themselves. Even characters that are supposed to be disliked need this kind of thing, to make them look real as opposed to being soulless puppets there just to move the story.

Reality, of course, um, you know, er, can go a bit; no, a tad ... or is it bit? Damned if I know, you know. Okay, my point is that too much reality, especially in dialogue, can be just as annoying as a wooden character. We all talk with a bunch of ums, ers, and ahs; adding that kind of thing, or vocally exact phrasing, might be real, but it also makes you want to throttle the speaker, not sympathize with them.

So, like a lot of things in writing, it's a balancing act. On one side is having characters that act as well as Kevin Costner and on the other is having dialogue and characters whose reality makes them confusing and frustrating (think David Mamet).

As a writer, I hope that they liked this article I just wrote, M. Christian thought.

CHAPTER 13: LOCATION, LOCATION, LOCATION

Even before writing about the sex in a sexy story, you have to set the stage and decide where this hot and heavy action is going to take place. What a lot of merry pornographers don't realize is that the "where" can be just as important as the "what" in a smutty tale. In other words, to quote a real estate maxim: location, location, location.

Way too many times, writers will make their story locales more exotic than the activities of their bump-and-grinding participants: steam rooms, elevators, beaches, hot tubs, hiking trails, space stations, sports cars, airplane bathrooms, phone booths, back alleys, fitting rooms, cabs, sail boats, intensive care wards, locker rooms, under bleachers, peep show booths, movie theaters, offices, libraries, barracks, under a restaurant table, packing lots, rest stops, basements, showrooms — get my drift?

I know I've said in the past that sexual experience doesn't really make a better smut writer, but when it comes to choosing where your characters get to their business, it pays to know quite a bit about the setting you're getting them into.

Just like making an anatomical or sexual boo-boo in a story, putting your characters into a place that anyone with a tad of experience knows isn't going to be a fantastic time but rather something that will generate more pain than pleasure is a sure sign of an erotica amateur.

Take for instance the wonderful sexual pleasure than can come from screwing around in a car. You haven't done it? Well, you should, because after you do you'll never write about it — unless you're going for giggles.

Same goes for the beach. Ever get sand between your toes? Now think about that same itchy, scratchy — very unsexy — feeling in your pants. Not fun. *Very* not fun.

Beyond the mistake of making a tryst in a back alley sound exciting, setting the stage in a story serves many other positive purposes. For instance, the environment of a story can tell a lot about a character — messy meaning a scattered mind, neatness meaning controlling, and so forth — or about what you're trying to say in the story: redemption, humor, fright, hope, etc. Not that you should lay it on so thick that it's painfully obvious, but the stage can and should be another character, an added dimension to your story.

Simply saying where something is happening is only part of the importance of setting. You have to put the reader there: details, folks.

Details! Research, not sexual this time, is very important. Pay attention to the world, and note how a room or a place *feels*. Focus on the little things that make it unique:

+ shadows on the floor or walls,
+ the smells and what they mean to your characters,
+ all kinds of sounds,
+ the way things feel,
+ important minutiae,
+ or even just interesting features.

After you've stored up some of those unique features of a place, use special and evocative descriptions to really draw people in. Though quantity is good, quality is better. A few well-chosen lines can instantly set the stage: an applause of suddenly flying pigeons, the aimless babble of a crowd, rainbow reflections in slicks of oil, twirling leaves on a tree, clouds boiling into a storm ... okay, that was a bit overdone, but you hopefully get my gist.

Once again: location is not something that's only important to real estate. If you put your characters into an interesting, well-thought-out, vividly written setting, it can not only set the stage for their erotic mischief, but it can also amplify the theme or add depth to the story. After all, if you don't give your writing a viable place, then a reader won't truly understand where they are — or care about what's going on.

CHAPTER 14: IDEA FARMING

It seems like every writer has some smart-assed answer to the age-old question: *Where do you get your ideas?*

For the longest time, I played with *the same place you'd get yours from, if you tried,* but it always sounds so arrogant, so superior. So now all I just give them a little, down-home reply: *Oh, from everywhere, I guess.*

For smut writers, the question is definitely more loaded than for other genres.

Do horror writers ever get the supposition that they hack up hitchhikers in the name of research? We merry pornographers, however, are automatically labeled perverts in real life simply because we have vivid sexual imaginations. Cut someone's head off, after all, and you only get an R rating—fuck them and it's XXX.

Still, I contend that story ideas for both come from the same place, and so deserve the same respect: the imagination. In most people, this tiny part of the cerebral cortex is pitifully underutilized, reserved for boss-murder and neighbor-fuck fantasies. For someone who likes to write, however, it's important to develop the imagination into a hefty piece of brain matter.

A common mistake a lot of beginning writers make is to think that creativity is something holy, untouched by outside influences. Fudge to that. Creativity is using what's around us in a new way, just like how every major work of art has its roots in everything else before it. I'm not talking plagiarism here, folks, but rather taking what's here and twisting it in your own unique fashion.

Not only can playing with existing forms in new and unique ways result in something wonderfully unusual, but also more importantly, it stretches your imagination muscle. Before you can twist, though, you have to stick something in your gray matter right next to your developing imagination: mainly that it's okay to dream.

Another common mistake is to think that everything you dream or play with has to have some kind of eventual purpose. Fudge to that, as well: *Play!*

Dream! Fantasize! Get *crazy*—you don't have to use everything you dream up, you don't have to write about everything you imagine. *Just have fun.* Your imagination, after all, is just like sex—if it's not fun, you're doing it wrong. So kick out that internal censor, and just allow yourself some good, old-fashioned chaotic dreaming.

Okay, so you've kicked your internal critic in the balls — so now what? Here's a great game: name a favorite movie. Go on, do it. Okay, so you're not a movie buff — how about a TV show, a book, a play, a comic book ... anything. Pick your fave. Got it? Now imagine a sequel, and write it in your mind.

You don't have to really write it, just play with what you liked about the original source and stretch it out. Say you love *Sunset Blvd.* Think about why you like it, what you want to see more of, what didn't work for you, what did, etc.

Now have fun! It doesn't have to be some great work of art, either. Pick what you like, look at why you like it, and then try and imagine something that incorporates it all. Sure it's tough, but remember: you're not going to actually do anything with it, just dream it up. Do something like this all the time. Another great technique is to watch a show or read a book and stop somewhere in the middle — and finish it yourself. Is your ending better? Is the original better? Why? Maybe how you ended it would make a better story — so take your new version and change it, add things you like, take out what you didn't. *Fun!*

Many people think I'm too hard on books and movies, that I'm too critical — but what's really going on is that, in my mind, I'm imagining a better movie or book. Friends are always kicking me in the shins when I groan in a movie, or rag on it endlessly afterward: *But it would have been so much cooler if they'd tied in the marriage with the funeral, so there's an echo of the loss — great foreshadowing!* I may never use what I'd been playing with, but every time that happens it stretches my imagination a bit more, making it easier to really dream when it comes time to face that blank computer screen.

This works for every genre, even erotica. There's sex all around us, subtle as well as obvious. As I've said before, often the difference between a good erotic story and a bad erotic story is *story!* Just a sex scene might be interesting, but it can never be anything beyond just interesting. But telling a story, with people ... that gets people's attention. A good way of farming for smut ideas is to look where sex is — and isn't, *yet.*

Look at *Sunset Boulevard* — we know that there's sex in that movie, even if it's just ... well, weird. If you take away the blink, it becomes a sex story, but one with a good *story.* I heartily encourage people to use their imaginations where good stories blink. *Fight Club*, for instance, has some delightful homoerotic moments — let alone the skid row sex with Marla. In your mind, fill in the blanks — not just sex for sex's sake, but with a sex scene that tells something about the character, the story, the setting. Just like you should finish stories, add to them. Show, if only to yourself, the rest of the story. Do that and I can all but guarantee your sex scenes will read more like fully realized characters being together, versus boring cardboard cutouts.

41

So get out your imagination, take it for a walk, feed it often, and— more than anything—play with it. Having a hearty, healthy imagination, after all, is what writing is really all about.

* * * *

Exercises:

1. Take a favorite book, movie, play, TV series (whatever). Got it? Okay now, in your mind or on the page, write a sequel to it. If that's too daunting try, instead, taking a TV show or movie and imagine what the book version would be like: how would it start? How would you describe the characters? Or, if you chose a book, create the film version in your head: cast the lead, decide what you might have to leave out of the story and what's essential. Remember: this is only an exercise, a way to get your creative juices flowing, so don't worry if your results aren't perfect.

2. Back to your favorite (fill in the blank) but this time pick something with a strong sexual subtext. Now make it not a subtext but instead a full-blown (ahem) sex scene. Particularly try to make the erotic details jive with what you know and understand of the characters. Sex is not a separate thing from life, remember: it shows as much of ourselves as does our walk, our choice in food, the way we talk.

3. Pick up a book, any book, or watch a movie or show or whatever but this time stop halfway through. Now create—again, either in your mind or on the page—an ending. Done? Now finish what the original. Was what you did better … or worse? If it was better then you have some you might want to twist, turn, change and/or expand into something your own. If the original was better then try to learn from it: what did the author (or film crew) do differently?

4. Go to the movies and watch the trailers, or the preview of coming attractions, or even the teaser for books. Now write your own story to go with what you'd seen. Try to imagine the opening, the introduction of the characters, the climax, the style, the ending. Try and get into the habit of doing this a lot. Before you know it your mind will be chugging away with all kinds of great ideas—erotic or not.

ASK A PROVOCATEUR: PATRICK CALIFIA

What makes a great erotic story?
This is a great question because I actually don't read much sexually explicit literature. So much of it is way too predictable. I look for some unusual characters that are well established. I want to be able to see these people and hear the unique quality of their speech. Then I want to see some kind of wrinkle in their approach to other people. And I really, really appreciate writers who can use language in an authentic way. Maybe that's a machine-gun of short, dirty, guttural words, or maybe it's elegant and polysyllabic. You can make vanilla sex as exciting to me as the most perverse BDSM scene if those two things are smokin'. And finally, I want the plot to surprise me. Writers who feel that sex is repetitive or predictable are going to produce lousy fiction. But if social sex-roles are violated, or the top/bottom dynamic gets flipped, or somebody turns out to want something we as readers didn't anticipate–that makes my hair stand up on end.

* * * *

What would you tell someone who is just starting out as an erotica writer?
I would honestly have to tell them that it is much, much harder now to get your work into print and get paid for it than it was twenty years ago. The Internet is a wonderful thing, but it's created the expectation that all entertainment will be free. Writers have been short-changed by this worse than the people who create visual images. Photographers and videographers have a better chance of getting paid than we do. The problem with this is that good writing—whether it's about sex or geography or politics—takes time. I have stories I've revised thirty times. You need the time to polish your rough draft into your best effort, pass it around to a good editor or three, get comments, consider them, integrate them, and then see what the final product is like. Do *not* take a job that is going to eat up all of your brain or leave you exhausted at the end of the day. Live simply or find a patron. (Patrons, remember, can be as time-consuming as a job. Make sure you have one who is low-maintenance.) Writing is so hard that you'll only make it if you devote your efforts to things that you feel compelled to put into words and push onto the screen or the page. Keep the people in your life who understand your priority is your writing, and ruthlessly eliminate anybody who makes fun of your work, shames you for it, or doesn't understand it. Cultivate the people who believe in you. And keep writing, every day, no matter what, let the words flow. Your voice matters.

43

* * * *

What's a common mistake writers make when writing erotica?

A common mistake is the idea that you can write something quick and shoddy, for easy money, without it affecting the rest of your work. First of all, there are very few gigs like that these days. Second of all, don't let yourself get into lazy habits or allow yourself to do less than your best. Another common mistake is to listen to that inner critic that says, you are awful and boring, you have nothing to say, you are not talented, this will never go anywhere, you can't talk about that, stop it, stop it, stop it. That voice is not your friend. And it will be there every fucking time you try to write, so develop a thick skin. That will come in handy for bad reviews and idiotic editors who hate writers. And the third most common mistake is to assume that only an editor can tell you if your work is any good. You see, most editors are failed writers. Very few of them are happy to be editors and want to nurture, protect, and develop their writers. Most of them want to smash up your soul and shit on your self-esteem. Editors are only good for signing checks. Never trust them. Paste a big smile on your face and fight them every inch.

* * * *

Patrick Califia is the author of *Mortal Companion, Hard Men*, and *Macho Sluts.*

CHAPTER 15: FLEXING

I'm astounded sometimes by writers who will only write one thing and one thing only: straight erotica, mysteries, science fiction, horror ... you name it. Their flute has only one note. They might play that one note very, very well, but they often neglect the rest of the scale. Not to go on about myself, but my own moderate accomplishments as a writer are the direct result of my accepting a challenge or two. I never thought I could write erotica—until I did. I never thought I could write gay erotica, until I did. Who knows what you might be great at? You won't know until you try.

A writer is nothing but pure potential, but only if that potential is utilized. If you only like writing straight erotica, try gay or lesbian. The same goes if you're queer: try writing something, anything, that you'd never in a million years think of doing. Maybe the story will suck, and that certainly does happen, but maybe it'll be a wonderful story or teach you something about your craft.

Challenge yourself. If you don't like a certain genre, like Romance, then write what your version of a romance story would be like. You don't like Westerns? Well, write one anyway: the Western you'd like to read. Of course, like a lot of these imagination games you don't have to sit down and actually write a Western novel. Instead, just take some time to visualize it: the characters, setting, some plot points, a scene or two. How would you open it? Maybe a tumbleweed blowing down a dusty street, perhaps a brass and black iron locomotive plowing through High Sierra snow? Or what about the classic Man With No Name staring down a posse of rabid outlaws? Who knows, you might be the best Western—or mystery, science fiction, gay, lesbian, straight etc.—writer there ever was, or maybe you'll just learn something about people, about writing. Either way, you're flexing, and increasing the range of your work.

This flexibility isn't just good in abstract: look at the books being published, the calls for submissions, and so forth. If you only like to write stories that one are particular style, flavor, or orientation, you'll notice you have a very, very limited number of places that would look at your work. But if you can write anything, then everywhere is a potential market. Write one thing and that's exactly how many places will want to look at what you do. Write everything and you could sell anywhere.

In other words: try! If you don't try, you won't know if you're any good. Some writers only do what they know and like because they don't want to face rejection, or feel they'd have to restart their careers if they change the one thing they do well. I don't believe any of that. If you can't handle rejection, then writing is not the life for you. Getting punched in the genitals by a rejection slip is part of the business, and something we all have to deal with. As far as a writer's career goes, no one knows what shape that'll take, or what'll happen in the future. Planning a job path in writing is like trying to roll snake eyes twelve times in a row: the intent might be there, but the results are completely chaotic. In the same way, a simple little story can turn out to be the best thing you're ever written, or an unexpected experiment can end up being a total artistic change.

Playing with new themes, genres, and styles is fun. Experiment on the page, in your mind, and who knows what'll pop up? Go to a bookstore and pick up something at random, read the back cover, and then spend a fun couple of hours imagining how you'd write it. What style would you use? What kind of characters? What settings? Even sit down and write some of it: a page, or even just a paragraph or two. It might suck, but that's the risk you always take trying something new — but it also could open a door to something *wonderful*.

* * * *

Exercises:

1. Pick a genre you either don't like or *really* don't like. Doesn't matter, really, what you pick — just pick something. Now write a book in that genre you actually might *like* to read. As with all these exercises you don't actually have to write the thing, you can only imagine it — with as much detail as you'd like. Do the same for all kinds of other media as well: movies, TV shows, plays, comic books, radio shows: create something you might find interesting.

2. Try to understand what about a certain genre you don't like — now try to work around that dislike. Say you don't like Westerns because female characters are always, or so you think, weak. Now write a Western with a great, strong female character.

3. Try melding apples and oranges. Creativity is not about plucking something from nothing, remember. It's often mixing and matching all kinds of crazy things. Create dice if you want to and roll them: horror and romance. Okay, now create your horror romance. Maybe boy meets zombie? Vampire gets the girl? Go nuts! So what if your result isn't great. This is all just practice to get your creative juices flowing freely.

CHAPTER 16: FETISH

Of all the things to write, I feel one of the all-time toughest has got to be fetish erotica. Gay or lesbian—or straight, if you're gay or lesbian or bisexual—is comparatively a piece of cake: just insert body part of preference and go with it. For gay erotica, it's a male body, and for lesbians, it's a female body. For straights, it's the opposite. You don't have to create the ideal man or woman; in fact, it's better to describe characters that are a bit more ... real. Perfection is dull, and can be bad storytelling, but a body with its share of wrinkles, blemishes, or sags can add dimension and depth.

The same goes with motivation, the inner world of your character. I've said it before, but it bears repeating: the trick to writing beyond your own gender or orientation is in projecting your own mental landscape into the mind of your character. You may not know how gay sex, lesbian sex, or straight sex feels, but you do know what love, affection, hope, disappointment, or even just human skin feels like. Remember that, bring it to your character and your story, and you'll be able to draw a reader in.

But fetishes are tougher. To be momentarily pedantic, Webster's says that fetishes are: "an object or body part whose real or fantasized presence is psychologically necessary for sexual gratification." That's pretty accurate—or good enough for us here—but the bottom line is that fetishes are a sexual interest that may or may not directly relate to sex. Some pretty common ones are certain hair colors, body types, smells, tastes, clothing, and so forth.

We all have them to some degree. To open the field to discussion, I like breasts. But even knowing I have that fetish doesn't mean I can really explain why I like big ones. It's really weird. I mean, I can write about all kinds of things, but when I try and figure out what exactly the allure of large hooters is for me, I draw a blank. The same thing (even more so) used to happen when I tried to write about other people's fetishes.

But I have managed to learn a couple of tricks about it, in the course of my writing as well as boobie pondering (hey, there are worse ways to spend an afternoon). I've come up with two ways of approaching a fetish, at least from a literary standpoint. The first to remember that fetishes are like sex under a microscope, that part of their power is in focusing on one particular behavior or body part. Let's use legs as an example. For the die-hard leg fetishist, their sexuality is wrapped around the perfect set of limbs. For a leg man, or woman, the appeal is in that slow, careful depiction of those legs. The sex that happens after that introduction may be hot, but you can't get away with just saying he or *she had a great set of gams.*

Details! There has to be details — but not just any kind of detail. For people into a certain body type or style, the words themselves are important. I remember writing a leg fetish story and having it come back from the editor with a list of keywords to insert into the story, the terms his readers would respond to and demanded in their stories. Here's where research comes in: a long, slow description is one thing, but to make your fetish story work, you have to get your own list of button-pushing terminology.

The second approach is to understand that very often fetishes are removed from the normal sexual response cycle. For many people, the prep for a fetish is almost as important, if not *as* important, as the act itself. For latex fans — just to use an extreme example — the talcum powder and shaving before even crawling into their rubber can be just as exciting as the black stretchy stuff itself. For a fetish story, leaping into the sex isn't as important as the prep to get to it. Another example that springs to mind is a friend of mine who was an infantilist — and before you leap to your own Webster's, that means someone who likes to dress up as someone much younger. For him, the enjoyment was only partially in the costume and role-playing. A larger part of his dress-up and tea parties was in masturbating afterward: in other words, the fetish act wasn't sex; it was building a more realistic fetish fantasy for self-pleasure afterwards. Not that all of your literary experiments need to be that elaborate, but it does show that for a serious fetishist, the span of what can be considered sex can be pretty wide.

The reason to try your hand at fetish erotica I leave to you — except to say what I've said before: that writing only what you know can lead to boredom for you and your readers. Try new things, experiment, and take risks. In the case of fetishes, it can only add to your own sensitivity and imagination — both in terms of writing and storytelling, but maybe even in the bedroom.

And who could argue with that?

CHAPTER 17: THE FOUR DEADLY SINS, # 1: UNDERAGE

Once in awhile someone will ask me "What, if anything, is verboten in today's permissive, literate erotica?" The answer is that pretty much anything is fair game, but there are what are called the four deadly sins: four subjects that a lot of publishers and editors won't (or can't) touch. These by no means are set in stone, but they definitely limit where you can send a story that uses any of them. So here, in a special series, are theses sins, and what – if anything – a writer can do with them.

* * * *

Of all the four deadly sins, the one that most-often cramps the style of many erotica writers (i.e. "pornographers") has to be the use of characters that are below the legal age of consent. The difficulties are multi-fold: every state and/or country has different definitions of both what consent is and the age that anyone can give it; very few people have actually lost their virginity when legally able to give consent (and having everyone in a story or book being twenty-one when they first have sex is just silly); and there's the scary potential that if you use a lot of characters below twenty-one you can look like a damned pedophile – and even get prosecuted as one.

Innocent scenes or even background like "he lost his virginity at seventeen" can be problematic, if not terrifying. While the likelihood is extremely remote, there still remains a chance that some Bible-thumping idiot from a backwater burg where consent is twenty-one could buy a copy of your work and then extradite you to said backwater to prosecute you for child pornography. It really has happened and could happen again. What really sucks is that they don't have to win their case to ruin your life: not only is suspicion as good as guilt to many people, but the legal costs alone are guaranteed to bankrupt anyone but Bill Gates.

So how do you avoid the wrath of Bubba from backwater creek? First of all, it really depends on how the story is written. While there's a chance they might go after you for that simple "he lost his virginity at seventeen" line, it isn't a big one. But if you do decide to write – and manage against all odds to sell, or at least publish – something that reads like a glorification of juvenile sexuality, your odds go up considerably. As with a lot of things, context and focus have a lot to do with it: anything sinful can be written about if it's done well and with an eye towards a finely crafted story with real emotion and dimension. James

Joyce was banned, but it didn't stick because it was art, and not *Catholic Schoolgirls in Trouble.*

Still, it's always better to be safe than sorry, especially since there are very simple techniques a writer can use to keep the law off his or her ass, or just keep a nervous editor or publisher from getting even more nervous. One of the simplest ways to avoid being accused of profiting off underage characters is to blur the specifics of the character's age. If I write, "he lost his virginity in high school," it could, technically, be argued that the kid had been held back for four years and had his cherry popped at twenty-one. No age, no underage. I've often been in the position where I've had to ask the author of a story to remove an exact age from a story to avoid just this issue. Most authors, once they understand the concern, are more than willing to make little changes like that.

Another place where age can slip in is through description. For example, if I say *boy*, that usually implies someone younger than a man, therefore below the age of consent. But if I use the word *lad*, the line gets fuzzy. Hell, I could say, "he was a strapping young lad of fifty summers" and get away with it. You can't do the same with *boy*—though of course you could say "young man." It's all subjective.

Of course, you can use *boy* in dialogue—as it could be a sign of domination or affection: "Come here, boy, and lick my boots." The *boy* in question could be sixty and graying. In one of those weird sexist twists of language, by the way, *girl* is not quite as loaded, as *girl* is frequently used to describe a woman of almost any age. Go figure.

Back to the high school thing: I don't want people to think you have to be incredibly paranoid to write erotica—but it is something to keep in mind. The Man (or even backwater versions of same) are hardly going to haul your ass off for just one line or just one story, but if someone goes go on a crusade, they sure aren't going to arrest the cast and crew of *American Pie* (or anything like it). You, maybe—them, definitely not.

Like all of these erotica-writing sins, the person who worries the most about these things isn't the Man or the writers, but the editors and publishers. Distributors are notoriously nervous around certain kinds of content, and these jitters are passed right down line to the publishers, and then to the editors.

Just as there are editors and publishers who are too cautious, there are others that don't care one whit, or even take pride in pushing as many envelopes as possible. You name the sin and they'll do it. While this is great, and deserves a hearty round of applause, it can also mean that if you write something really out there—even if it's something you think a market would like—and it gets rejected, you're stuck with a story that no one will ever look at. It's just something to keep in mind.

The answer to this confusion between the careful and the outrageous applies to most questions regarding markets for erotica:

+ read the publication,
+ check out the guidelines,
+ ask questions, and
+ don't argue.

I always remember this one person who sent me a story for a book I was editing, with an arrogant little note saying it was okay that the characters in his story were nine, because his story was set in Ancient Greece and the age of consent back then was eight. One, that was rude; two, I wasn't going to take anything with characters *that* young; and three, I didn't make the rules, the publisher did. I couldn't have taken the story even if I thought he was the next James Joyce. I didn't even read the story. I just rejected it.

In short, while it's not realistic — if not stupid — to insist that characters be legally old enough to have sex, it is a factor a writer should keep in mind. Write what you want to write, but the instant you make that decision to try and share what you write with the rest of the world, be aware that you're probably going to have to compromise or work within certain limitations.

It might not be pretty, but it's part of life — just like losing your virginity.

CHAPTER 18: THE FOUR DEADLY SINS,
2: BESTIALITY

Only in erotica can the line "Come, Fido!" be problematic. Unlike some of the other Four Deadly Sins of erotica writing, bestiality is very hard to justify: with few exceptions, it's not something that can be mistaken for something else, or lie in wait for anyone innocently trying to write about sex. This is unlike, for instance, discussing a first time sexual experience and have it accused of being pro-pedophilia. Bestiality is sex with anything living that's not human: if it's not living, then it's a machine, and if it was once living, then it's necrophilia.

A story that features—positively or negatively—anything to do with sex with animals is tough if not impossible to sell, though some people have accomplished it. However, there are some odd angles to the bestiality that a lot of people haven't considered—both positive and negative.

On the negative side, I know a friend who had an erotic science fiction story soundly slammed by one editor because it featured sex with something non-human, technically bestiality—despite the fact that there is a long tradition of erotic science fiction, most recently culminating in the wonderful writing and publishing of Cecilia Tan and her Circlet Press (both very highly recommended). Erotic fantasy stories, too, sometimes get the "we don't want bestiality" rejection, though myth and legend are packed with sexy demons, mermaids, ghosts, etc. This doesn't even get into the more classical sexy beasts such as Leda and her famous swan, or Zeus and other randy gods and demi-gods in their various animal forms.

Alas, "someone else did it" doesn't carry any weight with an editor and publisher, especially one that might be justifiably nervous about government prosecution or distributor rejection. Erotica, once again, gets—bad joke number three—the shaft: because erotica is up-front about the nature of its writing, alarm bells go off, unlike writing labeled scholarly or even pop-culture. Market something as erotic and the double standards start popping up all over the place.

On a positive note—as the already mentioned Cecilia Tan has proved—sex with aliens and mythological creatures has always been popular. Anthropomorphizing an animal and adding intellect or obvious will to a creature is a very safe way of touching on, or even embracing, the allure of sex with the unusual. The furry subculture is a close example of this, though they are very clear that this is not bestiality. It's just a way of eroticizing the exotic, mixing human sexuality with animal features. As long as the critters being embraced are not real animals and can give consent, then protests and issues usually fall away. Fantasy, after all, is one thing, and there's nothing more fantastic that dating a being from Tau Ceti V or something that looks like a raccoon crossed with Miss November, 1979.

There's another feature of bestiality that can be explored but only until recently has been: the idea of role-playing. In this take on it, a person will behave like an animal, usually a dog, and usually submissive. In these S/M games, the "dog" (notice that they are never cats) is led around on a leash, communicates in barks or whines, drinks and eats from a bowl, and is generally treated — much to his pleasure, or as punishment — like a pooch: read it one way and it's a unique power game, but read it another and it's bestiality.

One thing worth mentioning, because some people have brought this up in regards to all of the sins, is the *dream out*. What I mean by that is simple: say you really, really want to write about doing some member of another phylum. That's cool, but your chances of seeing it in print, or even on a Web site, are about slim to none. Science fiction doesn't turn your crank so you say: "Got it! It's a dream!" Well, I have news for you: a story that's slipped under the door with that framing device, as a way of getting about the idea of a *real* bestiality story apparent, especially when it opens with "I went to bed" and ends with "then I woke up" is a pretty damned obvious excuse to write an un-sellable bestiality story.

With a lot of these erotic "sins," whether or not a story comes across as being thoughtful or just exploitive and shallow depends a lot on how much you, as the writer, has put into the concept: something done cheap and easy will read just that way, versus the outcome if you invest time, thought, and — best of all — originality. Good work really does win out, and even can wash away some of the more outré' erotic "sins."

CHAPTER 19: THE FOUR DEADLY SINS, # 3: INCEST

Like bestiality—and unlike underage sexuality—incest is a tough nut: it's not something you might accidentally insert into an erotic story. Also like bestiality, it's something that can definitely push—if not slam—the buttons of an editor or publisher. Yet, as with all of these "sins," the rules are not as set in stone as you'd think. Hell, I even managed to not only write and sell an incest story ("Spike," which is the lead story in *Dirty Words*) but it also ended up in *Best Gay Erotica*. The trick, and with any of these erotic button-pushers, is context. In the case of "Spike" I took a humorous, surreal take on brother/brother sexuality, depicting a pair of twin punks who share and share alike sexually, until their world is shattered (and expanded) by some rough S/M play.

As with any of the "sins," a story that deals with incest in a thought-provoking or sideways humorous manner might not scream at an editor or publisher *I'M AN INCEST STORY*. Instead, it will come across as humorous or thought-provoking first, and as a tale dealing with incest second. Still, once it comes to light, there's always a chance the story might still scream a bit, but if you're a skilled writer telling an interesting story, there's still a chance quality could win over the theme.

Unlike bestiality, incest has very, very few *stretches* (like aliens and myths with bestiality). It's very hard to stumble into incest. In short, you're related or you're not. As far as degree of relationship, that depends on the story and the intent: immediate family relations are damned tough to deal with, but first cousins fooling around behind the barn are quite another.

Even though incest is pretty damned apparent in a story, that doesn't mean the theme or the subtext can't be touched on. Sometimes the forbidden or the unexpected lying under the surface can add depth to a story: a brother being protective of his attractive sister, a mother shopping for a date for a daughter, a father trying to steer his son's sexuality, a daughter's sexual explorations alarming (and enticing) a mother or father's fantasies, and so forth. Technically, some of these dip into incest, if not the act then at least the territory, but if handled well they can add an interesting facet to an otherwise mundane story. It's a theme that's also been played with, successfully, for centuries. Even the myth of Pygmalion—a sculptor falling in love with his creation—can almost be considered a story of incest, as the artist was a parent, then a lover.

Conversely, incest can dull a situation when the emotions of the lovers involved become turned: as an example, where a person begins to feel more of a caregiver or mentor than a partner: the thought or even fantasies around sexuality with the person being cared-for or taught start to feel inappropriate. Conversely, someone might enjoy the forbidden spice of feeling sexual towards someone they've only thought of as a son or daughter, mother or father figure. This is also an old plaything for storytellers, the most common being a person looking for a partner to replace the strength and nurturing left behind when they grew up and moved out—or, from the new partner's point of view, the shock in realizing they have been selected to fulfill that role.

As with any of these "sins," fantasy can be a factor in being able to play with these themes. Having a character imagine making love to their mom (shudder) is in many editors or publishers eyes the same thing as actually doing it—but accepting and using the theme in, say, play-acting, where the reality is separated because the participants aren't related in any way, is more acceptable. As with under-age play, S/M and dominance and submission games can also use incest as a spice or forbidden theme—especially in infantilism games, where one person pretends to be an abusive or nurturing parental figure. Once again, play versus reality (even imagined reality) can work where normally no one would dare tread.

The bottom line, of course, is whether or not the story is using this theme in an interesting or thought-provoking way, or just as a cheap shot. If you have any questions, either try and look at the story with a neutral eye, or ask a friend you respect for their opinion. But I wouldn't ask your parents.

CHAPTER 20: THE FOUR DEADLY SINS, # 4: VIOLENCE

In regards to the last of erotica's sins, a well-known publisher of sexually explicit materials put it elegantly and succinctly: "Just don't fuck anyone to death." As with the rest of the potentially problematic themes I've discussed here, the bottom line is context and execution: you can almost anything if you do it well — and if not well, then don't bother doing it at all.

Violence can be a very seductive element to add to any genre, let alone erotica, mainly because it's just about everywhere around us. Face it, we live in a severely screwed up culture: cut someone's head off and you get an R rating, but give someone head and it's an X. It's kind of natural that many people want to use some degree of violence in their erotica, more than likely because they've seen more people killed than loved on-screen. But violence, especially over-the-top kind of stuff (i.e. run of the mill for Hollywood), usually doesn't fly in erotic writing. Part of that is because erotica editors and publishers know that even putting a little violence in an erotic story or anthology concept can open them up to criticism from all kinds of camps: the left, the right, and even folks who'd normally be fence-sitters — and give a distributor a reason not to carry the book.

One of the biggest risks that can happen with including violence in an erotic story is when the violence affects the sex. That sounds weird; especially since I've often said that including other factors are essential to a well-written erotic story. The problem is that when violence enters a story and has a direct impact on the sex acts or sexuality of the character, or characters, the story can easily come off as either manipulative or pro-violence. Balancing the repercussions of a violent act on a character is tricky, especially as the primary focus of the story. However, when violence is not central to the sexuality of the characters but can affect them in other ways it becomes less easy to finger point — such as in noir, horror, etc — where the violence is background, mood, plot, or similar without a direct and obvious impact on how the character views sex. That's not to say it isn't something to shoot for, but it remains one of the harder tricks to pull off.

Then there's the issue of severity and gratuitousness. As in depicting the actual sex in sex writing, a little goes a long way: relishing in every little detail of any act can easily push sex, violence, or anything else into the realm of comedy, or at least bad taste. A story that reads like nothing but an excuse to wallow in blood — or other body fluids — can many times be a big turn-off to an editor or publisher. In other words, you don't want to beat a reader senseless.

But the biggest problem with violence is when it has a direct sexual contact. In other words, rape. Personally, this is a big button-pusher, mainly because I've only read one or two stories that handled it ... I can't really say *well* because there's nothing good about that reprehensible act, but there have been a few stories I've read that treat it with respect, depth, and complexity. The keyword in that is *few*: for every well-executed story dealing with sexual assault there are dozens and dozens that make me furious, at the very least. I still remember the pro-rape story I had the misfortune to read several years ago. To this day, I keep it in the back of my mind as an example of how awful a story can be.

Sometimes violence can slip into a story as a component of S/M play. You know: a person assaulted by a masked intruder who is really (ta-da!) the person's partner indulging in a bit of harsh role-play. Aside from being old hat and thoroughly predicable, stories like this can also fall into the "all pain is good pain for a masochist" cliché, unless, as with all things, it's handled with care and/or flair.

Summing up, there is nothing you cannot write about: even this erotic "sin" or the others I've mentioned. However, some subjects are simply problematic in regards to sales potential: themes and activities that are loaded with emotional booby traps have to be carefully handled if the story is going to be seen as anything other than a provocative device. The affective use of these subjects has always been dependant on the writer's ability to treat them with respect. If you have any doubts about what that might be, just imagine being on the receiving end: extrapolate your feelings as if one of your own personal traumas or sexual issues was used as a cheap story device or plot point in a story. Empathy is always a very important facility for a writer to develop — especially when dealing with sensitive or provocative issues.

In short, if you don't like being beaten up, then don't do it to someone else, or if you do, then try and understand how much it hurts and why. Taking a few body blows for your characters might make you a bit black and blue emotionally, but the added dimension and sensitivity it gives can change an erotic sin, something normally just exploitive, to ... well, if not a virtue, then at least a story with a respectful sinner as its author.

CHAPTER 21: DRIVE

A friend of mine once called me ambitious. I'm still not sure what he meant by that—was it a compliment or criticism? Put-down or praise? It's made me think, though, and that's always a good thing. I'd normally describe ambition as a drive to succeed, a persistence to rise in status, income, reputation, so forth. But what does that mean to a writer? It could be money—but since when is money the answer to anything? It could be reputation—but then a lot of bad writers are well thought of, even famous (are you listening, Tom Clancy?). Ambition can also mean cold-heartedness, or a reckless disregard towards anything and anyone that's not directly related to a goal.

God, I hope I'm not that.

I do know that writing is important to me—probably the most important thing in my life. Because of that, I look for opportunities to do it, and to get it seen. I rarely let opportunities pass me by: markets, genres, experiments—anything to get the spark going, juice up my creativity, and get my work published. Erotica was one of those things, an opportunity that crossed my path and it has been very good to me. I didn't think I could edit a book, but then I had a chance to do that as well, and now have done a bunch of the suckers.

The fact is that opportunities never find you: *you have to find them.* The fantasy of some agent, or publisher, or agent, picking up a phone and calling you out of the blue is just that: a fantasy, or so rare it might as well be just a fantasy. Writing is something that thrives on challenge, growth, and change. Some of that can certainly come from within, but sometimes it takes something from the outside: some push to do better and better, or just different work. Sending work out, proposing projects, working at maintaining good relationships with editors, publishers and other writers is a way of being involved and getting potential work to at least come within earshot. It takes time, it certainly takes energy, but it's worth it. The work will always be the bottom line, but sometimes it needs help to develop, get out, and be seen—those contacts and giving yourself a professional push is often what it takes.

Remember, though: Ambition can also mean "a cold-heartedness, a reckless disregard towards anything and anyone that's not directly related to a goal." Drive is one thing, but when it becomes an obsession with nothing but the politics of writing and not the work itself, it takes away from the process rather than adding to it. Being on both sides of the fence—as an editor as well as a writer—I know how being determined and ambitious can either help or hinder in getting your work out. Being invisible and hoping for opportunity won't get you anything but ignominy. However, if you're pushy, arrogant and care only for what someone can do for you and not that you're dealing with a person who has their own life and issues, you can end up closing doors rather than opening them.

I like working with people who know about Chris, and not just the person who can publish their work—just as I like writing for publications that are run by kind, supportive, just-plain-nice folks. Rejections always hurt, but when that person is someone I genuinely like or respect, then I'll always do something better next time. As I've said before, writing can be a very tough life and having friends or connections that can help, both professionally as well as psychologically, can mean a world of difference. Determination to be published and to make professional connections at the cost of potential comrades is not a good trade-off. I'd much rather have writing friends than sales, because in the long run having good relationships is much more advantageous than just the credit. Books, magazines and web sites come and go, but people are here for a very long time.

But more than anything else, it's vital to never sacrifice the love of writing or the struggle to create good work. Someone can have all the friends in the world and a black book full of agents and publishers, but if they're lazy or more concerned with getting published than doing good work, they are doing those friends and markets, as well as themselves, a serious disservice. Getting out there is important, and determination can help that, but if what gets out there is not worthy of you ... well, then why get out there in the first place? It might take some time, might take some work, but good work will usually find a home: a place to be seen, but bad work forced or just dumped out there is no good for anyone, especially the writer.

The bottom line, I guess, is that I really do believe in ambition, both for work and to find places to get exposed, but more importantly I believe in the bottom line: the writing. The drive to be a better and better writer is the best kind of ambition of all.

ASK A PROVOCATEUR: CATHERINE LUNDOFF

What makes a great erotic story?

A great erotic story is composed of many of the same elements that make for any kind of great story: believable, interesting characters, an interesting plot and well-drawn settings, with, of course, the added bonus of hot sex. "Hot" is relative, but all good erotica shares many of the same characteristics, including sexual tension and chemistry between the characters. There are myriad ways to depict that connection, ranging from eye contact to the brush of shoulders or hands against each other to detailed fantasies. All help to give the reader something to relate to and to pull them into the story. Even when a story is more sensual than graphic, the reader should be able to imagine a next step, regardless of whether or not it's on the page. The beauty of writing good erotica is that you can directly impact your readers and get them hot and bothered, as well as providing fantasy fodder for future dreaming.

* * * *

What would you tell someone who is just starting out as an erotica writer?

Always present your best work. If you are sending a story to a themed anthology or publisher, your story should be related to the theme. Don't send your sweet heterosexual romance to a publisher who specializes in gay BDSM. Make sure that your story adheres to the publisher or editor's guidelines and that it is formatted correctly and thoroughly proofread. The more professional your work is, in terms of both quality and appearance, the better for your career in the long run.

* * * *

What's a common mistake writers make when writing erotica?

The assumption that I run across most is two sides of the same coin: either it's so incredibly easy to write erotica that anyone can do it, or its opposite, that writing about sex is the most terrifying thing ever and they could never do it. The truth, for most writers anyway, lies somewhere in between. Erotica can be difficult to write well, but is certainly not impossible. Read other authors in the genre that you want to write in and study what they do, good and bad. Learn something about anatomy — the Good Vibrations and Cleis guides are an excellent starting place. Write until you get comfortable with the kind of sex you want to write about; practice makes better, if not perfect.

* * * *

Catherine Lundoff is an award-winning author and editor. Her most recent book is her collection, Night's Kiss: Lesbian Erotica *(Lethe Press, 2009).*

CHAPTER 22: WALKING THE LINE

There's no doubt about it, things are really tough right now: aside from the depression/recession that seems to be killing publishers daily — and making life even harder for writers — there's the too-often-painful transition from print to digital books, and the problem of getting yourself heard in a world full of other authors screaming for attention.

So it's only natural that writers would feel a lot of pressure to write books and stories to fit what they think is the flavor-of-the-moment, to work only to spec.

So, should you do it? In my opinion the answer is a definitive, absolute, certain ... kind of.

Before getting too far into it, I should back up a tiny bit and say that stories are very different — *no duh* — critters than novels. Aside from the obvious length thing, the big difference between the two is that with stories getting the out into the world usually depends on if you're writing for a specific anthology, Web site, and such. If that's the case then, absolutely, you should work to try and meet the guidelines set by the publisher or editor.

But even then you can be too specific, follow the guidelines too literally. It goes like this: you sit down and create the perfect story for a project — one that you've carefully crafted to be exactly what the editor is looking for. The problem, though, is that a lot of other writers are more than likely doing exactly the same thing, so when they all arrive on the editor's desk you could very well be just one of a dozen perfect stories.

The trick is to step onto the tightrope between being exactly what the editor wants and unique enough to stand out. Alas, this is easier said than done, but there are a few important things to remember that can make it a tad easier to pull off. First of all, always respect the editor's plan for the book: if they are reading for, say, a vampire book, then don't send in a werewolf story. Second, being unique doesn't mean using the book as a personal platform: even though you might hate vampires, try to write a story that respects the genre and its readers. Thirdly, the best way to stand out from the pack isn't by being audaciously outré, but instead by writing a unique but still accessible story — a new twist, but not something completely warped.

Hey, I never said it was easy. There's something else to always keep in mind when you're trying to walk that very thin line between mundane and outrageous: you're taking a risk. If you're lucky, then yours will be the story that stands out from the rest of the submissions on the editor's desk, or be the one in the book that everyone talks about. If you're unlucky, though, then you'll get a rejection slip.

Tough, I know, but here are worse things than rejection — and this is the same for both novels as well as stories. Sure, you can create something designed from word one to fit the flavor of the moment but you'll be doing everyone, especially yourself, a real disservice: approaching everything you do with only an eye to riding the wave will mean that your work will always just be part of something else, that you'll never stand out. My favorite story about this comes from a few friends who used to write classic porn — cheap bumpy-grindy stuff. After a few years of so-called-success, they woke up one day suddenly realizing they'd become soulless, lazy writers and couldn't do anything else.

All this, however, is not to say you never should pay attention to what's out there or never try your hand at writing for a specific market. Aside from the reward of possibly getting your work out there, trying new things — even trying to be the next flavor of the month — is how writers discover hidden talents or may even find they enjoy writing a certain kind of story or book.

Before closing, I should go back to that difference between stories and novels (again, aside from the length). Stories are always worth an experiment. Novels, though, are a tougher call, as there's a lot more at risk — months instead of a few days. But it also could be argued that writers should take bigger risks with novels than stories because of that investment, because it's hard enough to stand out at all, let alone when you're novel was written to be just like every other one in the genre.

In the end it all comes back to the tightrope, to finding a balance between playing it safe and being unique. One wrong step and you might be too different to be popular, or not even get out there at all, or fall the other way and be yet another copycat book in a fading genre — or trap yourself into being a common, bland, lifeless hack.

Yes, there are tricks and things to keep in mind when you step onto that line but the best teacher, as always, is experience. You will make mistakes, we all do, but with practice you'll hopefully find what every writer hopes to find: not success (because that word really has no meaning), but instead a balance between art and commerce, between paying-the-bills popularity and admirable literature.

CHAPTER 23: PEDDLING YOUR ASS

The inclination is obvious, especially considering how much pressure writers can be put under to get themselves out there. But even though I call myself a Literary Streetwalker, I want to take a few hundred words to talk about when, in my opinion, it's not a good idea to sell your creative backside.

One of the coldest rules of being an erotica author is that it's a sexist genre: women have a slightly easier time of it than do guys—unless you're penning gay stuff, of course. Straight men still remain the primary buyers of erotica, and they usually don't enjoy stuff written by men. Is this homophobic? Certainly. But them's the breaks until our society grows up. Women also don't seem to trust anything written by a man, being suspicious that a man can't write about sex. Is this wrong? Absolutely. But again, that's simply the way the world works—for the moment, at least.

In this world of literary female domination, some women authors have made the mistake of selling themselves rather than their work. The temptation, like I said, is clear: turning yourself into a desirable product makes it easy to sell just about anything you do, whether it's a book or your own underwear. Becoming a sex personality means that you carry your catalog with you; you don't have to trouble yourself with showing people what makes you a writer worthy of reading.

There are other benefits as well. Celebrity has a special allure. There's nothing like the adrenaline rush of people saying you're sexy or clapping when you walk on stage. Writing, as I've said many times before, is a spectacularly harsh mistress. With the low pay, generally poor treatment, and little artistic recognition, it's no wonder that so many women are seduced by the quick and easy fame—or at least recognition—of becoming a product or personality, rather than a writer.

Now I should qualify what I mean by "selling." I'm all for writers marketing themselves and their work. Becoming an expert on something is an established marketing technique and lots of people do it very well, but there's a huge difference between becoming an authority and actually peddling your ass: if you write articles and essays on sex and sexuality, or give advice on it, then you're an expert; talk about who you took to bed last night and you're selling yourself.

There are two good reasons for not crossing that line between publicity and soliciting. The first is more professional: if you create yourself as a sexual superstar, you're severely limiting what you can do as a writer. Your sex life might get you attention, but walk away from that spotlight and you'll find yourself in the dark: your audience having been used to you as a sex object, not as a writer, and won't respond when you're not writing about being a pro-dom, sex activist, or porn star. Flexibility, after all, is key to being a writer because it gives you a plethora of genres and venues in which to expand and play. Your erotica didn't sell? Try horror. Horror didn't work? Try romance, and so forth. Unless, that is, you turn yourself into nothing but a sex object — then that's all you can be.

If you want to turn yourself into a sexual superstar, don't let me stop you: it's your right as a free person. But I sincerely recommend that you resist the temptation to market yourself and not your work. Besides being a potential dead end career-wise, the other reason for not writing about your own sex life and putting it out there for hundreds, maybe thousands and — who knows? — millions of people to read: *fans*.

Not to put down the handsome and well-groomed reading world, but way too many of my female writer friends tell me that having die-hard admirers of their sexual personas, rather than their stories, is more a curse than a blessing — and really, really creepy. I'd say unwelcome advances are another reason to write stories about all kinds of things, and not about how wonderful it was jerk off the entire swim team.

CHAPTER 24: VALUE

Money, bucks, dough, dollars, legal tender, the green stuff: I've got some news for ya, folks. Being a writer, you are just not going to be seeing a lot of it.

I know that's tough to hear, but that's the reality. The number of folks who make even just a living wage at writing is too damned small. Hell, I can't do it. In fact, no one I know can do it, and I know quite a lot of writers. The few that come close are usually pretty high on the profile scale: lots of novels, screenplays, those kinds of really big things—and then a lot of those big things.

Not that writing for a living is impossible, but I find way too many folks start out writing thinking that being Stephen King and million dollar advances are right around the corner. The spiel I usually give about writing and money is that it's possible to make money, fun money, but it just isn't enough to live on.

It's true in erotica as in other genres—even though, yes, sex sells. But what shocks beginning erotica writers even more than the lack of funds coming their way is this: to writers, especially erotica writers, money isn't all that important.

Now, wait a minute; I don't mean that writers shouldn't get paid, or that payment shouldn't be fair. What I mean is that money, for a beginning writer, shouldn't be a major motivation for either writing or deciding where to submit a story for consideration.

For instance, just like everywhere else in life, money does not equal quality. Lack of it, not being paid a lot, does not mean a publication is not worthy of your work. Similarly, a high-paying market doesn't mean a quality book, magazine, or Web site.

When building a body of work, while money is nice—very nice—it's most often not what other writers, publishers, and editors will notice when they look at your cover letters. Saying that you have stories in *Big Boobs Monthly, Leathermania V,* or *Transsexual Hookers in Trouble* might mean lots of green backs, but it doesn't spell high quality. Though if you say your work has appeared on a quality and respected site, it might not mean dinner out and a show but it does mean: *wow!* Respected sites and magazines may not pay, but their editors know a good story when they read one, so to have passed their scrutiny can be worth more than a nice big check.

Sure, I think everyone should get paid — especially if the editor or publisher is taking a lot of money home and not sharing with the contributors involved — but sometimes money is not the only way a writer can be paid. Not to sing the same song too many times, but making connections can often lead to much bigger deals, markets, and opportunities down the road, and only looking at an editor or publisher by what they pay may mean missing much more valuable opportunities later on.

But that doesn't mean that a writer should throw their work away. Very often I come across writers who desperately want to see their work in print — or on a Web site — and so will post or send off their work to the first opportunity without first trying it somewhere nicer. Nicer, of course, doesn't mean big bucks but rather better status or acting as a way to find better gigs. I really recommend writers start out high: try for a book, or a print magazine, or a really superb site before settling for something with not a lot of visibility just to get your story in print, so to speak. It might mean facing rejection (in fact it usually does) but it's better to try for something big then settle for something small, in life as well as in writing.

If I could sum this up in a simple statement, I guess I'd say that it's important to remember that your work always has value, even though value doesn't always equal money.

CHAPTER 25: THE ONLY WINNER...

So ... contests. In a word: don't!

(sigh) What is it with you people? Can't you just accept the word of an internationally renowned literary authority and acclaimed sex symbol?

Yes, I mean me. Who else do you think I'm talking about?

Okay ... okay ... I guess I'm going to have to spell it out for you (sigh again). So here goes:

I've been seeing a lot of these things lately: send in your stories for this or that competition, and the winner gets published and (sometimes) a bit of cash. The worst of them — and clearly the ones to completely, totally avoid — are the ones that require a fee to enter.

But even the contests that don't make you pay to play are bad for writers (which means all of you) and bad for writing, in general. Sure, entering a contest might, at first, sound like a good idea: you get to say you won this or that competition, giving you a chance to put a blue ribbon on your resume or in your bio.

But let's think it through. Writing is hard. Getting a single story published in a magazine, on a Web site, or in an anthology is difficult. Do you need the added pressure of trumping dozens if not hundreds of other writers for a little recognition of (in most cases) dubious authenticity? The odds are not only ridiculously against you, but the rewards are questionable.

It gets worse. Say I'm doing an anthology on ... oh, I don't know, sex-on-a-train stories. To get in, you have to submit a well-written story related to that topic. Rarely, if ever, are contests that specific. Most of them are so ambiguous you'll have absolutely no idea what they are looking for, let alone who actually might be making the final decision and what kind of storytelling they might favor.

Again, think of the odds. To a writer, time is money. Do you seriously want to waste the time it takes to write — or even submit — a story to a contest versus writing something that may, actually, have a chance of getting accepted and published?

Okay, a lot of folks don't write something new for a contest; most will simply pull something out of their files. But even then, I still think entering a contest is a bad idea. A very bad idea.

Why? Call it part of a personal crusade. Writers always seem to get the short end of the stick — and what's even worse, we seem to be happy with that short stick, accepting it as our professional lot in life. We get paid very little for a lot of work, far too often have to deal with unqualified editors and publishers, and have to keep going against catty reviews and miniscule pay. Now, a lot of these things won't be fixed by staying away from contests but think of it this way: are you respecting yourself by entering the shark tank that's a competition?

Besides, these days even winning a competition means pretty much zilch. There are so many of them, and so many that are practically worthless, that even being able to hang that blue ribbon on your career means virtually nothing. As an editor, I can't tell you the number of times that a story has been submitted that is … well, in need of a lot of work. But the author has won an award. It's getting to the point where awards mean that the winner was either the best of half a dozen runner-ups or got themselves a ribbon because their circle or community knew them and not the other entrants.

But the bottom line is that contests really serve one—and only one—purpose, and it's not to help writers. Competitions are a cheap way to get a person, a Web site, or a magazine a grand dollop of promotion and publicity without having to pay a dime to anyone but the winner. It's viral marketing under the guise of literary acclaim. Meanwhile, the contest sponsors get all kinds of content that they didn't have to pay for but from which they will find a way to profit.

You are a writer. That's a very special thing. Yes, you have to deal with the realities of what that means but there's no reason why you have to enable people who are only trying to take advantage of your determination and passion. So the next time an invite for a contest drops into you're in box earn yourself a blue ribbon by doing what's good for you, as a writer: hit Delete.

ASK A PROVOCATEUR: CAROL QUEEN

What makes a great erotic story?

First, character/s that get my attention. Second, sex that is hot and authentic to that/those character/s — even if the character is doing that sexual thing for the first time. I care about the psychology *and* the erotic experience, and the best stories get me into people different from me and let me go along for their sexual ride. Third, writing that is skilled enough not to detract from the experience of reading.

* * * *

What would you tell someone who is just starting out as an erotica writer?

Don't do it because you think sex sells and you'll make a lot of money — most erotica writers aren't rolling in dough, but rather do it because they adore the opportunity to delve into sex in their writing. Instead of self-censoring and worrying about going too far, the assignment is often to go as far as possible! — and in doing so, we can inform, educate, inspire, turn on, support, and become really important literary friends to our fans. This is exciting, enriching, and it's also a lot of responsibility. Which leads me right to your next question!

* * * *

What's a common mistake writers make when writing erotica?

Some erotica writers really only write from their own experience, and many do it beautifully. But I can't tell you how many stories I've seen where it's pretty obvious that the writers did not know what they were talking about, and simply fantasized their way into a scenario, or drew characters so shallow or stereotyped as to be pretty offensive. Erotica is political and has social importance, because sex in our culture is politicized and not everyone has access to information, support, and community to live a sexually healthy life. So when you write about *anything*, I think it's your responsibility to be as educated as possible about that form of sexuality, the body parts and psychology involved, and write as though your reader's own erotic feelings and identity are at stake (or their beliefs about other people's). Pat (now Patrick) Califia is my hero in this regard, and I hope everything I write is worthy of the inspiration I received from him when I began to write.

* * * *

Carol Queen has a PhD in sexology, which she uses to impart more realistic detail to her smut. She is founding director of the Center for Sex & Culture and a much-published author/anthologist.

CHAPTER 26: FACTS OF LIFE

It can be very weird being an editor as well as a writer. It's definitely a kind of schizophrenia, being on both sides of the fence at once: spending the morning rejecting other writers' stories and then crying myself to sleep when it happens to me. Schizophrenia? Actually it's more like a kind of bad sex: mornings fucking someone, and then getting fucked myself. Kind of appropriate for erotica writing and editing, no?

While I completely agree that good work will always win out, there is a certain amount of packaging that is needed to get the work to the editor so that it arrives with a smile and not a grimace. And, speaking from experience, sometimes a frown or a grin can be the difference between acceptance or rejection.

Manuscripts are not resumes. The trick with resumes is to catch the eye, to get yours stand out above the rest. Career counselors often recommend bright colors and tricks to get the potential employer to spot a resume in a pile of potentials, but manuscripts are exactly the opposite. With a manuscript you want the work to be the only thing the editor notices, not that you printed the story on bright red paper, or that you used a teeny-tiny font. Anything that gets in the way of the editor reading what you have written is a strike against you. Now no real editor will reject a story just because you didn't know about Standard Manuscript Format but if reading the story is a chore—or you neglected important information with the submission—you might look to be too much trouble to deal with. Remember, there are usually dozens of other stories sitting on that editor's desk, just waiting to be easier to deal with or read.

By the stories I've been getting, I think I'm a bit of a fossil; I still put my stories in a Standard Manuscript Format. It's basically very simple, but I like it both as a writer and an editor because it gives all the important information needed to read a story, and contact the writer, in one neat package.

Even though it sounds simple, you'd be surprised at the number of stories I get that don't have any of this.

Your name, address, and contact information. This is obvious—it's how the editor reaches you if he wants your story, or sadly doesn't. Even if it's already in your email, definitely put your name and address in your manuscript as well. You'd be surprised how often stories get separated from their cover letters.

The word count. This is very important: it gets me annoyed, for example, to get a story without a word count and then not realize that it's way too long for the book I'm working on, after reading through most of it. So put in a word count, for sure: rounded to the nearest hundred, by the way.

A cover letter. Unlike some editors I know, I like cover letters: they can tell a great deal about the person I might have to work with. A good cover letter should be brief, pleasant, professional, and include a SHORT listing of where you've been published. If you haven't been published, please don't say that: some editors have an anathema against virgin writers. I don't know about other editors, but I hate just getting a URL instead of a list of credits, even in an email submission. I have crappy web-access at home and have been annoyed way too often by Web sites full of prancing kittens and java flames when all I was looking to see if the writer was a pro or not (obviously not).

My advice if you're stretching the guidelines a bit for a submission (say the word limit is 4,000 and you have something that's 5,000 or so) is, above all else, be polite. Recognize you're pushing the limit of the book, and apologize if that's not appropriate.

Just a few more things: email is a necessity nowadays, so make sure you have a good, consistent one. There's nothing worse than trying to reach someone for an acceptance only to have the message bounce. The same goes for your snail-mail address. I recommend a good Post Office box or mail drop: sometimes editors can take years to get back to you with the good news or bad, and if you move and can't be found ... well, how will you get the contract?

That's the basics: the pragmatic facts of life in regards to packaging up your work. Now get out there, have lots of fun, write terrific stories, and send them out. I wish you the very best, and that the editor you work with will see your submission as great work — and not as that weird manuscript with the pink type, the rude cover letter ... and where the hell is the word count?

[STANDARD MANUSCRIPT FORMAT]

REAL First & Last Name
VERY permanent mailing address:
(PO Box or Mail Service)
City, State Zip
Phone (though not required)
VERY permanent email address
(NO social security number)

Approximate word count

(Eight spaces)

Story Title (Title Case)

By

Real name or pseudonym

(Three spaces)

Start the story here, with a paragraph indent of .2. Use courier 12

point, double-spaced. You can also use Times. Two spaces after each

period. One space, two hyphens -- like this -- for a dash. For italics, you

underline. No bolding, no strange fonts, no "fancy footwork" typography: the idea is for a seamless transition from story to editor's brain.

Be sure to have a header on each page with your name (or pseudonym), the story title, and the page number. Even if you're sending the story as an attachment to an email a lot of editors still print out their submissions to read them—and no editor wants to try and figure out what page goes where if your story happens to get jumbled when it comes out of their printer.

No spaces between paragraphs. For a parenthetical break (like a scene change) use one return, a symbol, then back to the story, like this:

#

Then back to what you were doing. No playing with formats: multiple columns, indenting, and so forth -- you can, of course, but if it gets in the way of the story or might cause problems for publication then a lot of editors will just toss the manuscript aside as being too hard to deal with.

Small typos are okay, but try and keep the first pages as clean as possible -- a bad mistake in the first line or paragraph can label a writer as sloppy, which is not a good thing. If you spot a mistake, correct it and print out a new copy of the manuscript rather than trying to edit an existing copy.

Get a good and quick printer or have access to one. When you get to the end of a story, just be traditional and use something like:

The End

CHAPTER 27: HOWDY

Writing the story is the most important element of getting your book published, but there's something right below that: drafting an effective cover letter—or cover email, as this is a digital age.

So here is a quick sample of what to do and not to do when putting together a cover letter to go with your story. That being said, remember that I'm just one of many editors out there, each with their own quirks and buttons to push. Like writing the story itself, practice and sensitivity will teach you a lot, but this will give you a start.

* * * *

So ... Don't Do What "Bad Johnny Don't" Does:
Dear M. (1),

Here is my story (2) for your collection (3), it's about a guy and a girl who fall in love on the *Titanic* (4). I haven't written anything like this before (5), but your book looked easy enough to get into (6). My friends say I'm pretty creative (7). Please fill out and send back the enclosed postcard (8). If I have not heard from you in two months (9) I will consider this story rejected and send it somewhere else (10). I am also sending this story to other people. If they want it, I'll write to let you know (11).

I noticed that your guidelines say First North American Serial rights. What's that (12)? If I don't have all rights then I do not want you to use my story (13).

I work at the DMV (14) and have three cats named Mumbles, Blotchy and Kismet (15).

Mistress Divine, Goddess of the Multiple Orgasm (16)
Gertrude@christiansciencemonitor.com (17)

* * * *

(1) Don't be cute. If you don't know the editor's name, or first name, or if the name is real or a pseudonym, just say "Hello" or "Editor" or some such.

(2) Answer the basic questions up front: how long is the story, is it original or a reprint, what's the title?

(3) What book are you submitting to? Editors often have more than one open at any time and it can get very confusing. Also, try and know what the hell you're talking about: a collection is a book of short stories

by one author, and an anthology is a book of short stories by multiple authors. Demonstrate that you know what you're submitting to.

(4) You don't need to spell out the plot, but this raises another issue: don't submit inappropriate stories. If this submission was to a gay or lesbian book, it would result in an instant rejection and a ticked-off editor.

(5) The story might be great, but this already has you pegged as a twit. If you haven't been published before don't say anything, but if you have then definitely say so, making sure to note what kind of markets you've been in (anthology, novel, Web site and so forth). Don't assume the editor has heard of where you've been or who you are, either. Too often, I get stories from people who list a litany of previous publications that I've never heard of. Not that I need to, but when they make them sound like I should, it just makes them sound arrogant, which is not a good thing.

(6) Gee, thanks so much. Loser.

(7) Friends, lovers, Significant Others and so forth—who cares?

(8) Not happening: I have a stack of manuscripts next to me for a project I'm doing, and the deadline for submissions is in two months. I will probably not start reading them until at least then, so your postcard is just going to sit there. Also, remember that editors want as smooth a transition from their brain to your story as possible; anything they have to respond to, fill out, or baby-sit is just going to annoy them.

(9) Get real—sometimes editors take six months to a year to respond. This is not to say they are lazy or cruel; they're just busy or dealing with a lot of other things. Six months is the usual cut-off time, meaning that after six months you can either consider your story rejected or you can write a polite little note asking how the project is going. By the way, writing rude or demanding notes is going to get you nothing but rejected or a bad reputation—and who wants that?

(10) When I get something like this I still read the story, but to be honest, it would take something of genius-level quality for me to look beyond this arrogance. Besides, what this approach says more than anything is that even if the story is great, you are going to be too much of a pain to work with. It's better to find a story just as good from someone else than put up with this kind of an attitude.

(11) This is called simultaneous submission: sending a story to two places at once, thinking that it will cut down on the frustration of having to wait for one place to reject it before sending it along to another editor. Don't do it, unless the Call for Submissions says it's okay, of course. Even then, though, it's not a good idea because technically you'd have to send it to two places that think it's okay, which is damned rare. The problem is that if one place wants your work, then you have to go to the other places you sent it to in order to tell them so—which very often results in

one very pissed editor. Don't do it. We all hate having to wait for one place to reject our work, but that's just part of the game. Live with it.

(12) Many editors are more than willing to answer simple questions about their projects, but just as many others will never respond — especially to questions that can easily be answered by reading a basic writing book. Know as much as you can and then, only then, write to ask questions.

(13) This story is automatically rejected. Tough luck. Things like payment, rights, and so forth are very rarely in the editor's control. Besides, this is a clear signal that, once again, the author is simply going to be way too much trouble to deal with. Better to send out that rejection form letter and move onto the next story.

(14) Who cares?

(15) Really, who cares?

(16) Another sign of a loser. It's perfectly okay to use a pseudonym, but something as wacky as this is just going to mark you as a novice. Also, cover letters are a place for you, as a person, to write to the editor, another person. Put your pseudonym on your story, but don't sign your cover letter with it.

(17) Email address — this is great, but it's also very obviously a work address, which makes a lot of editors very nervous. First of all, people leave jobs all the time, so way too often, these addresses have very short lives. Second, work email servers are rarely secure — at least from the eyes of prying bosses. Do you really want your supervisor to see your rejection from a *Big Tits in Bondage* book? I don't think so.

* * * *

Do What Johnny Does Does:

Hi, Chris (1),

It was with great excitement (2) that I read your call for submissions for your new anthology, *Love Beast* (3). I've long been a fan not only of werewolf erotica (4) but also your books and stories as well (5).

I've been published in about twelve Web sites, including *Sex Chat, Litsmut,* and *Erotically Yours,* and in two anthologies, *Best of Chocolate Erotica* (Filthy Books) and *Clickety-Clack, Erotic Train Stories* (Red Ball Books) (6).

Enclosed is my 2,300 word original story, "When Hairy Met Sally" (7). I hope you have as much fun reading it as I had writing it (which is a lot) (8). Please feel free to write me at smutpeddler@yahoo.com if you have any questions (9).

In the meantime best of luck with your projects and keep up the great work. (10)

Molly Riggs (11)

* * * *

(1) Nice; she knows my real first name is Chris. A bit of research on an editor or potential market never hurt anyone.

(2) It's perfectly okay to be enthusiastic. No one likes to get a story from someone who thinks your project is dull.

(3) She knows the book and the title.

(4) She knows the genre and likes it. You'd be surprised the number of people who either pass out backhanded compliments or joke about anthologies or projects thinking it's endearing or shows a 'with it' attitude. Believe me, it's neither: it's just annoying.

(5) Editing can be a lonely business, what with having to reject people all the time. Getting a nice little compliment can mean a lot. It won't change a bad story into an acceptable one, but making an editor smile is always a good thing.

(6) The bio is brief, to the point, and explains the markets. You don't need to list everything you've ever sold to, just the key points.

(7) Everything about the story is there: the title, the words, if it's original or a reprint—and, of course if it's a reprint you should also say when and where it first appeared, even if it's a Web site.

(8) Again, a little smile is a good thing. I know this is awfully trite but when the sentiment is heartfelt and the writer's sense of enjoyment is true, it does mean something to an editor. I want people to enjoy writing for one of my books, even if I don't take the story.

(9) Good email address, obviously not work, and an invitation to chat if needed. Good points there.

(10) Okay, maybe it's a bit thick here but this person is also clearly very nice, professional, eager and more than likely will either be easy to work with or, if need be, reject without drama.

(11) Real name. I'd much rather work with a person than an identity. I also know that Molly is not playing games with who she is, and what she is, just to try and make a sale.

There's more, as said, but this at least will keep you from stepping on too many toes, even before your story gets read. If there's a lesson in this, it's to remember that an editor is, deep down, a person trying to do the best job they can, just like you. Treat them as such and they'll return the favor.

ASK A PROVOCATEUR: CECILIA TAN

What makes a great erotic story?

When an author picks a really scorching erotic moment to focus on, from a deeply internal point of view that will get my panties sopping much faster than a lot of description of sexual gymnastics. You need to spend just as much talent and craft on making it HOT as you do on all the other writerly things you do, like making the characters three-dimensional and pacing a good plot, etc.

* * * *

What would you tell someone who is just starting out as an erotica writer?

Decide right now whether you are going to be an activist whose erotic works help society move towards better sex and better love lives in the future, or whether your erotica will perpetuate the 'sex stays in the closet' mentality. I realize that coming out as an erotica writer for many people is just as potentially harmful in terms of social stigma, potential lost jobs and child custody, etc. ... as coming out as gay. Which is exactly why it's important that more people come out.

* * * *

What's a common mistake writers make when writing erotica?

One of the most common is trying to go back and forth between two characters' points of view. It's incredibly difficult to do well, and with the close-in intimate narrative stance that tends to work best for erotica, it's horribly jarring to have been in one character's head all along and then suddenly in the sex scene find out what the other person in the scene is thinking or feeling. You think you are writing "omniscient" narrator, but trust me, you're not. Stick with one character's point of view within scene.

* * * *

Cecilia Tan is the author of many books that mix the erotic with the fantastic, including *Mind Games, The Siren and the Sword, White Flames, Black Feathers*, and *Edge Plays*. She is the founder and editorial director of Circlet Press.

CHAPTER 28: THE CARE AND FEEDING OF EDITORS

As I've mentioned before, in many ways, I'm a queer beast—in the literary world, especially, because I'm an editor as well as a pretty prolific writer. I know the biz from both ends, as someone rejecting as well as getting rejected. Wearing my editorial sombrero, I've noticed a trend in the stories I've been reading ... professional annoyances, pains in the derriere, pissing-off things, and just plain rude stuff that I thought I might vent ... er, ah, *share* with you. This also gives me a chance to explain how to deal with editors—though, as with anything in professional writing, it's very subjective. This is stuff that I consider important, or frustrating, etc., but another editor might feel completely differently about.

Before I get to the bits and piece of a submission, a bit of philosophy: despite how much writers hate it, an editor has no professional obligation to be nice, respond in a certain amount of time, give comments on a rejection, or answer any questions. The only time that changes is when a story has been accepted, and even then, there are no hard and fast rules. The worst that can usually happen is an editor getting a bad name, or getting a protest lodged against them with the National Writers Union. Getting ignored by or frustrated with an editor is just part of the game. The sooner a lot of writers realize that, the sooner they'll make some real professional progress. Conversely, it's very frustrating for an editor who tries their best to be polite, professional, and sympathetic to end up on the receiving end of some neurotic writer's wrath: in short, roll with the bad and applaud the good—kind of a good life philosophy, too, ain't it?

In that regard, it's never a good idea to ask a lot of an editor. Simple questions ("What's your deadline?" "Who's your publisher?" "What's your pay rate?" and so forth) are fine, but asking an editor to write, even if it's returning a post card, or a call just to let you know the manuscript came through okay are not: facing a huge stack of unread manuscripts to read, accept or reject, the last thing an editor wants to do is deal with more paperwork. Besides, an editor often doesn't open an envelope until they're ready to read—sometimes months after they've received it.

Politeness counts a huge deal. Often I'll be extra polite or conscientious to a writer if they've been understanding and nice to me. I'll always respond (or try to), but a demanding email or a cover letter dripping with arrogance is definitely a lower priority compared with someone who starts out: "I know you're really busy—" or "Absolutely no rush, but I'd be grateful if—" and so forth. Like writers, a lot of editors just a little want kindness and respect: treat them that way and you'll get a much better reaction. Start off with the assumption that they are being intentionally rude (as opposed to busy, dealing with a family emergency or who knows what) and you'll usually get a rude response right back—as well as being burned into the editor's mind as a "demanding jerk"—which can damage how they might read your work in the future.

Even though you may not get a polite response, always take the high road and start out that way. Yeah, it's not fair to be polite to someone who's rude, but getting into a hissing and spitting match won't win you any battles. Besides, we editors *talk to one another*: being rude to a friend of mine will eventually get around to me, and vice versa. Which is also a way of dealing with someone who has treated you unfairly: tell your writing buddies—warn them if a certain editor is tough, or bad, to work with. Knowing ahead of time that an editor is slow, always rude, easy to annoy and so forth can save a lot of hassle, frustration and self-doubt if you or anyone else decides to work with them in the future.

If you happen to get rejected—and it will happen—in a particularly rude way then don't fall into the trap of acting out, being spiteful. Like I said, editors talk to each other, so if you write a nasty letter back, or post a catty review of the editor's books on some site or other, all that's going to happen is you're going to get not just that one editor's door slammed in your face but possibly many others. I don't like the way some editors treat authors but that doesn't mean I condone attacks on them or their other books. Unfortunately, being a writer means having to do a lot of cheek-turning; if you can't handle that, then find another line of work.

Now then, for some little things—cover letters, for instance: I like cover letters because they give me a clue as to the personality of the person I might be working with. Ideally, a cover letter should be professional, short, and give an editor the impression that the writer is going to be easy to work with. A bio is essential, but only share what's important to your writing life. The fact that you work for the DMV, have five cats, and build model ships in your spare time is interesting—but not to me or any other editor. By the way, if you've never written before, or never for the genre or market you're submitting to, don't say it. After all, would *you* feel good about your doctor saying, "You know, I've never done something like this—but I think it came out well"?

Something I've mentioned before but absolutely have to say again: pick a snail-mail address and an email address that you can live with for *a very long time*. I am very, very tired of trying to reach a certain writer only to have their addresses bounce (both surface mail as well as email). Remember, if an editor can't find you, they can't accept you—no editor is going to spend valuable time trying to hunt you down. You get one, maybe two, rarely three shots — after that you just end up in the "rejected but can't contact" pile. Also, if you submit anything via email be sure your story has all your contact info on it — no editor is going to dig through dozens (if not hundreds) of emails trying to match yours with a certain story.

While I'm fuming, let me toss off a few more pet peeves:

When sending reprints, do not just photocopy the book or magazine the story first appeared in (*you* try reading a bad photocopy);

Be sure to remember to put on the manuscript its number of words (which can be a deal-killer if the editor suddenly realizes the story's way too long);

Do not submit a story to two books or magazines simultaneously — there's nothing worse that getting a book put together and then find out that a writer sold the story you just bought to someone else;

Don't start haggling over things likes rights or fees until you've been accepted (besides, the editor rarely decides that kind of stuff, anyhow);

If you don't have an email address then get one — too much business is conducted these days via email, especially when deadlines (rewrites, editorial questions and so forth) have gotten to be days rather than weeks or months; and while I'm on the subject of email, please check your mail at least once a day — it can be very frustrating to try and reach someone only to have them spend weeks to get back to you.

Anyway, thanks for this space and time to let me, in my editorial chapeau, to share some thoughts and frustrations – in order to make up for my usual venom I promise in my next Streetwalker installment to reverse it all and talk about how to work with editors and publishers from a writer's perspective.

In the meantime: Get a good email account and stick with it!

Sheesh!

CHAPTER 29: THE CARE AND FEEDING OF WRITERS

Editing can be a lot like parenting: far too often it seems like the people who are shouldn't have been. Okay, that's definitely a bit harsh — I'm just a sucker for a good opening line. Still, while there are lots and lots of great editors out there (and you know who you are — or should) there are some who have been burned indelibly into the minds of many writers: the literary equivalent of *Mommie Dearest*. With that in mind, I'm going to take this opportunity to write an open letter to my fellow editors out there about the game, as seen by someone who plays for both sides.

It's very easy to forget that there is a person on the other side of a story submission, especially when that submission irritates you in some way. You are buried under a ton of stories that are inappropriate, demanding, or just plain bad, and a dismissive style is damned tempting. Still, try to think of each story as a person with his or her own hopes and dreams, good points and bad. That doesn't mean you have to take them home, tuck them in bed and read them a bedtime story — hardly. But they do deserve respect and politeness whenever possible. Try to answer their questions and concerns or deal with their silly issues as you would want yourself treated: promptly, courteously, and professionally. As with lots of things in life, giving good will get the same right back.

Rejection is part of the job. If you can't reject someone, then find another line of work. Not responding to a submission is not rejecting it; it's just insensitive. It's painful, it's hard, but a price of having your name on a book — or on the staff of a magazine or Web site — is having to send out that awful "Dear Author" letter. It's never easy, and sometimes it really smarts — especially when it's someone you know or an author you respect — but it has to be done. My advice for softening the blow for everyone concerned is to make your rejection notice as friendly and conscientious as possible: thank them for their story, mention how hard the decision can be in selecting stories, say something positive (anything at all) and wish them the very best and encourage them to keep writing. I know some editors who think that being completely honest is the best thing. Not to give writers false hopes or inflated egos, but I also know a lot of those same editors don't like their own reality pointed out (overweight, thinning hair, bad breath, etc.). The fact is that writing is damned hard: writers put their egos and their souls on the line every time they send a story out. To not acknowledge that bravery, to not respect and acknowledge it, is cruel — not honest.

Never forget that while your name appears on the book or as part of an editorial staff, you didn't write the stories. It's good to feel proud about a book you've put together — and god knows editors get damned little praise as it is — but never forget that you're just the ringmaster, not the wirewalker or the clown or the acrobat. To get back to the parental analogy, and stretch it a bit too far, don't be a stage mother taking credit for your little Tiffany tap-dancing her brains out. Without writers, a book, magazine, or Web site is nothing, so never forget the people who made it all possible: the individual writers and even those who tried but didn't make the cut. After all, a side effect of being hard to work with, editorially, is a diminishing pool of writers willing to work with you. Today's rejected author might very well write next year's "best story ever" — if you make them feel safe trying again.

Despite what I said previously, sometimes the truth is best. For instance, it's much better to be honest and say that you're running late, got buried under stories, or have other projects that are on tighter deadlines and so forth when someone inquires as to the fate of their story — much better than, say, not answering. Being honest that things are crazed, or things have gone wrong, is much better than leaving some author fretting or scratching their head. Most authors are very understanding and sympathetic when you admit being buried or stressed — while no one likes to be ignored or dismissed.

Being sensitive to the feelings of authors can come in many forms. I still wince about being put on the mailing list for a certain anthology — one that I'd been rejected from several times. Ah, there's nothing like reading rave reviews and heaped-on praise for a project you didn't get into to bolster the ego.

My personal rule as an editor is to try and leave them … well, if not smiling, at least not crying. Being abrupt, rude or insensitive to an author will get you nothing but someone who will frown, growl, or at least wince whenever they see your work. Not to sound Machiavellian, but that's not a very smart way to do business: the writing life is very unpredictable — today's lowly contributor to an anthology is tomorrow's agent, reviewer, celebrated author, or even another editor. Leaving unnecessarily hurt feelings behind you will come back to haunt you, guaranteed.

In editing, as in life, it's better to make friends and not enemies: being sympathetic and supportive will serve you very well — because who knows when you might be on the other side of the fence.

CHAPTER 30: PAPERWORK

You've written a story — *congratulations!* — sent it out for consideration to a magazine, or anthology — *bravo!* — and then suddenly you get a letter: "Thank you for your submission. We are pleased to say that we enjoyed your story and would like to publish your story. Please sign the two copies of the enclosed contract, keep one for your records and send the other back to us as soon as possible."

Now what?

After the giddying wash of euphoria and the call to your mother, you take a look at the contract — and are instantly, and totally, confused. Welcome to the world of professional writing.

To say that contracts can be baffling is an understatement. Clauses, terms, rights, royalties, and the whole kit and caboodle seem designed more to confound and baffle rather than be clear about what the hell you're putting your name and Social Security number on. But there is some good news in navigating the maze of legalese that surrounds giving permission for a publisher to use your work.

The first bit is that not all contracts are written in Sanskrit. Some can even be brutally direct, laying out what they want and what you're agreeing to in very simple language. Unfortunately, these short and sweet contracts can be pretty rare.

But even the more complex agreements basically boil down to a few key things to watch out for. The top of the list is the idea of *Rights*: what the publisher is buying from you. I'll discuss the two major kinds:

1. First Serial Rights, or One Time Rights, and
2. All Rights.

The most common is called First Serial Rights, or One Time Rights. Now I'm not a lawyer (I'm warm blooded), but my rule of thumb is that in most cases this means that the publisher — through the editor — wants to use your story one time, and then the rights revert back to you. This means that after it appears in the publication you can sell it elsewhere, just as long as you tell the next editor or publisher that it was printed somewhere else, and where that was. Some contracts specify for how long you have to hold onto your story before trying to sell it again, but that's pretty unusual. Still, respect any time limit mentioned — you don't want to piss a publisher off for no damned good reason, or because you were impatient.

Rarely some publishers want what's considered All Rights. The trick here is that you are basically selling your story to the publisher. Your work will no longer belong to you, so you can't sell it anywhere else—or not without the publisher's permission. The good news is that when a publisher wants this, they usually pay a handsome hunk of dough. If they don't, think twice about signing anything. For example: you sell a story one time First Serial Rights for $50, and then manage to sell it again for $100, and then maybe even $250 down the road. That story has now earned $400. If you'd sold that story for All Rights for only $200, you would have lost out on a lot more money, as well as lots more exposure. Thankfully, publishers who want All Rights are pretty rare—I've only seen it twice in ten years of selling stories, so it isn't something you really have to worry about.

Like I said, I'm not a lawyer and not even that good about dealing with paperwork—which will probably annoy quite a few of you considering I'm writing here about contracts and such. But to be honest, even though I don't know a clause from a term, I have managed to plow through contract red tape with some success. The big thing to remember is to win the war, not necessarily the battle. When a contract crosses my desk, I look for the rights being purchased—or rented—and anything *really* suspicious. But that doesn't mean I call up the editor and rant and rave about the terms. Rarely does an editor have any say in what the contract says. Most of the time contracts are created by the publisher, set by some lawyer or other, and are usually not something that can be tweaked.

I'm not saying you shouldn't protect yourself or sign something you feel uncomfortable with, but what I am saying is to recognize the reality of the situation. The editor wants a seamless transition from sending out contracts to turning in the final book. The publisher wants the same: manuscript to printer to the stands. They do not want someone writing or even worse calling them up saying that they are "uncomfortable" or confused by a contract. I hate to say this, but in terms of fiction writing, authors are a dime a dozen. A lot of publishers or editors will simply reject or recall an acceptance rather than deal with a pain-in-the-ass author. The key word is *fiction*, by the way; for serious non-fiction authors or freelancers, I would seriously recommend reading up on contract terms and so forth, as a publishers using and then re-using is much more common for non-fiction than for fiction.

None of this means you don't have any power in a contract situation. Some editors and publishers will actually accept agreements with line edits—contacts with clauses lined out or altered—though keep in mind that, as far as I know, such contracts aren't binding until you get a signed agreement. Just lining out something already signed by an editor or publisher (which is very common) doesn't mean that anyone agreed to those new terms, no matter how much you hope it does.

Like I said, I'm not an expert on contracts and such. If you are uncomfortable with anything, paperwork wise, please talk to other writers—especially ones that have worked with the editor or publisher you have the concern about—or consult some more authoritative sources of info: Try the National Writers Union, for example, or pick up a copy of *Writer's Market*. A lot of stress and fear can be alleviated by finding out if a publisher is really evil (as their contract seems to be), or if they have hearts of gold but just weird paperwork.

The bottom line though is that you should always do what's right. Always remember that getting your way on paper is only good if you can keep getting your stories published. Becoming a jailhouse lawyer that jumps on everything that doesn't meet an over-exact, paranoid standard that an editor can't change and a publisher won't change isn't going to get you anything—especially another contract.

ASK A PROVOCATEUR: SAGE VIVANT

What makes a great erotic story?

If there's one thing I learned from operating Custom Erotica Source for 10 years, it's that there is no absolute answer to this question. Eroticism is in the eyes of the reader. For me, less sexual detail and more emotional tension makes for a sexier tale, but for many readers, every juicy physiological detail is important. (Admittedly, readers who fall into this category are often the ones surfing the Internet for a quick fix. Good literature is probably not high on their list of priorities. If a writer chooses to write for that audience, though, they'll want to keep the story focused on sex, get to the action quickly, and describe it so that reader feels like they are part of the story.) Personally, I find overwrought descriptions of the sexual act supremely boring and even skip over them when I read erotica. For me, such descriptions are like watching porn that zooms in on genitals. Yuck. I want a story that's about more than sex. One cannot underestimate the power of plot and human emotion.

* * * *

What would you tell someone who is just starting out as an erotica writer?

Don't expect to live on this income! Also, friends and family are always going to tell you that your work is hot and sexy and deserves to be published. They are frequently being kind. Learn to write erotica as you would learn to write any other fiction: pay attention to character development, story arcs, and use of language. Just because it's erotica doesn't mean that it can't be high quality literature. Many new writers feel the mere fact that they're writing about engorged body parts and wild desires makes the story compelling, but that's really not true. I've always found that stories that put sex before all else miss the mark. There are no surprises in such stories, and as a result, the reader gets bored.

* * * *

What's a common mistake writers make when writing erotica?

Thinking that readers are going to love what you wrote for your significant other. They won't. Honest. Write something else for people you're not sleeping with.

* * * *

Sage Vivant is the author of the novel *Giving the Bride Away* (Fanny Press, 2009) and the book *Your Erotic Personality* (Berkley Books, 2007). With M. Christian, she has edited several anthologies, including *Confessions, Amazons, Garden Of The Perverse*, and more. Her short stories have appeared in dozens of anthologies and can be heard on Playboy Radio.

CHAPTER 31: KEEPING IT TOGETHER

Well it's tax time again, and I'm here to tell you to do something I didn't do for the longest time, and, no, it's not making out a yearly check (sigh) to the IRS. I mean keeping track of what you're up to.

It may seem a bit left-brain for all you good right-brain writers, but keeping organized and maintaining accurate records is very important for a writer, and not just to keep the audit wolves from huffing and puffing down your door.

As you write more and more stories—and hopefully get more and more serious about sending them out—keeping track of what went where and when becomes essential. Even the most left-brain of you right-brains can't always remember what story went to what editor and, most importantly, when it was sent out. Just to paint you a vivid picture, here's a common situation: you know you shipped off "Busty Nurses in Trouble" to *Big Tit Magazine,* but can't remember when that was—and so you sit longer than you should on the story and miss out on other opportunities. Or you don't remember what story you sent. Or you think you sent it off a long time ago and, pissed, you berate the editor only to realize you just sent the story off a week or two before. Red faces, for sure, but in this business a wrong impression can take a long time to wear off.

Instead of guessing or plowing through your sent email folder, it's much wiser to create a simple database or table or all your work and when/when/how/why and so forth it was sent you. For all your technophiles I suggest Excel, and for the Luddites I recommend a simple MSWord table. You don't need a lot of info for your records, but I've always found that more is always better. Or, I should say, more is better since I learned to keep good records. There's a point to this; just be patient.

Here are some of the basics things to put into a database and why they are such a good idea:

Story title: duh.

Words: because sometimes a market is only interested in stories of a certain length, or more/less than a certain length.

Subject Matter: I recommend a simple code, like gay, straight, S/M, Fetish, and so forth. The reason for this is that certain markets want certain things, and it's way too easy to forget what you've written. You can also sort by this code in certain programs so you don't have to plow through record after record looking for a certain type of story. Just click and there they all are. Neat-o.

Submitted When/Where: If you're like me and certain stories just won't sell, then you'll need a lot of these, one for each unsuccessful attempt. It might be depressing to fill it out for the sixth or seventh time, but it's better than sending the same story to the same agent twice. Trust me on this one.

Published When/Where: Always a good idea to keep track, just in case a new market is not interested in reprints, or vice versa.

Paid: It does happen—believe it or not—so it's good to keep track of how much (if anything) you got and when the check came. If you also want a really good cry, just total up this field to see exactly how much you've made.

Notes: For whatever else you want to say about a story.

Those are the basics, but feel free to add a lot more—some folks, for instance, like to put in editor's addresses, how the story was sent (email vs. snail, for instance), and all kinds of other stuff.

The other kind of record keeping that you should be mindful of should be obvious by the way I started this column: money, coming in for sure, but especially going out. Now I'm not an accountant and wouldn't even play one on television, but I do know that you should keep track of everything and then let your professional play with it. Depending on your tax situation, you can sometimes deduct such unlikely expenses as:

+ ISP fees,
+ all of your postage,
+ DVD and CD purchases,
+ mailbox rentals,
+ office furniture,
+ phone bills and more.

Like I said, it's really up to your accountant, but if you don't keep good track of it all, how are they even going to know where to start? It's better to over-keep records than not at all.

How do I know? Well, I haven't been audited (knock on wood) but I have had the experience where I've sent a story to an editor only to have them reject it with a note: "I didn't like this the first time I read it." This is a big bummer and a lesson for writers everywhere, especially me.

CHAPTER 32: EMOTIONAL SURVIVAL KIT

Please read this if you just had something rejected:

It's part of being a writer. Everyone gets rejected. Repeat after me: *Everyone gets rejected.* This does not mean you are a bad writer or a bad person. Stories get rejected for all kinds of reasons, from "just not the right style" to a just plain grouchy (or really dumb) editor. Take a few deep breaths, do a little research, and send the story right out again or put it in a drawer, forget about it, remember it again, take it out, read it, and realize it really is damned good. Then send it out again.

Never forget that writing is subjective. My idea of a good story is not yours, yours is not his, and his is not mine. Just because an editor doesn't like your story doesn't mean that everyone will, or must, dislike it as well. Popularity and money don't equal quality, and struggle and disappointment don't mean bad work. *Keep trying. Keep trying. Keep trying.*

Think about the rewards, about what you're doing when you write. I love films, but I hate it when people think they are the ultimate artistic expression. Look at a movie—any movie—and you see one name above all the others: the director, usually. But did he write the script, set the stage, design the costumes, act, compose the music, or anything really except point the camera and tell everyone where to stand? A writer is all of that. A director stands on the shoulders of hundreds of people, but a writer is alone. Steinbeck, Hemingway, Austen, Shakespeare, Homer, Joyce, Faulkner, Woolf, Mishima, Chekhov—all of them, every writer, created works of wonder and beauty all by themselves. That is marvelous. Special. That one person can create a work that can last for decades, centuries, or even millennia. We pick up a book, and through the power of the author's words, we go somewhere we have never been, become someone new, and experience things we never imagined. More than anything else in this world, that is true, real magic.

When you write a story, you have created something that no one—no one—in the entire history of history has done. Your story is yours and yours alone; it is unique and you, for doing it, are just as unique.

Take a walk. Look at the people you pass on the street. Think about writing, and sending out your work: what you are doing is rare, special, and damned brave. You are doing something that very few people on this entire planet are capable of, either artistically or emotionally. You may not have succeeded this time, but if you keep trying, keep writing, keep sending out stories, keep growing as a person as well as a writer, then you will succeed. The only way to fail as a writer is to stop writing.

But above all else, keep writing. That's what you are, after all: a writer.

* * * *

Please read if you just had something accepted:

Big deal. It's a start. It's just a start. It's one sale, just one. This doesn't make you a better person, or a better writer than anyone else out there trying to get his or her work into print. You lucked out. The editor happened to like your style and what you wrote about. Hell, maybe it was just that you happened to have set your story in their old hometown.

Don't open the champagne; don't think about royalty checks and huge mansions. Don't brag to your friends, and don't start writing your Pulitzer acceptance speech. Smile, yes; grin, absolutely, but remember this is just one step down a very long road.

Yes, someone has bought your work. You're a professional. But no one will write you, telling you they saw your work and loved it; no one will chase you down the street for your autograph; no one will call you up begging for a book or movie contract.

After the book comes out, the magazine is on the stands, or the Web site is up, you will be right back where you started: writing and sending out stories, just another voice trying to be heard.

If you write only to sell, to carve out your name, you are not in control of your writing life. Your ego and your pride are now in the hands of someone else. Editors and publishers can now destroy you, just as easily as they can falsely inflate you.

It's nice to sell, to see your name in print, but don't write just for that reason. Write for the one person in the whole world who matters: yourself. If you like what you do, and enjoy the process: the way the words flow, the story forms, the characters develop, and the subtleties emerge, then no one can rule what you create, or have you jump through emotional hoops. If a story sells, that's nice, but when you write something that you know is great—something that you read and tells you that you're becoming a better and better writer—that's the best reward there is.

But above all else, keep writing. That's what you are, after all: a writer.

CHAPTER 33: WHY NOT?

Every writer gets frustrated, especially when they've been rejected for stories that seem to be just what the editor was looking for: smart, stylish, deep, interesting, heartfelt, and all the rest. It was a sure winner, right?

But first, a quick word about rejection slips. Do they really express how the editor feels about your work? No, they don't. Now, that doesn't mean that some editors aren't being sincere when they send out their rejections—especially if they include a personal message with their generic rejection—but it's just about impossible for one editor to write to everyone who didn't make the cut. What's their answer? Enter the form rejection letter. They can be polite ("Sorry, your story didn't meet the needs of our publication"), cold ("Your submission was not satisfactory"), sympathetic ("I know how tough this is") or even rude ("Don't you EVER send me this drivel again") but they mean the same thing: *better luck next time.*

But there is a bright side. Think of it this way: at least that editor spent the time to send those notes out. There are still some cowardly editors out there who never reject; you just hear that your friends were accepted or the book comes out and you're not in it. At least getting a note—any note—means that you can now send the story somewhere else.

Now then, onto the Great Secret of Being Accepted. Are you ready? You sure? Okay, okay, put the baseball bat down. The Great Secret of Being Accepted is ....

There isn't one. If there were, don't you think I'd be selling it? If there were, then why the hell do I still get rejected? The fact is that even though you think, hope, and work really hard to give editors exactly what they want, the decision is still very subjective. In my own case, I've been rejected because:

+ The story is too long by a few hundred words
+ The editor didn't get aroused reading my story
+ There is already a story selected that's set in New York City
+ The editor doesn't like the use of certain words in a story
+ The publisher may object to it
+ Some of the sex is "objectionable."

Now I've never used any of these reasons—either subconsciously or consciously—in rejecting a story, but that's just me. Every editor is unique, as are the criteria for taking, or not taking, a story. At first, that seems like a situation that should, nay must, be corrected somehow, but that's just the way the world works. The editor is the boss, and he or she is trying to put together the best book they can, using what stories they got, according to their own call for submissions. If there was a concrete method for selecting stories, we'd have books by machine, and anthologies created by a precise formula. Luckily for the reader, we don't, but this lack of a more scientific — or at least quantifiable — method for picking stories can be very frustrating for the writer.

If it helps, rejection never gets any easier to give or to get. As an editor, I hate to give them out, but I have to because I feel writers deserve to know whether they made the cut. I'm also in a position of having to put together the best anthology, as I see it. As a writer, I still get rejection notices and will get even more in the future. It's simply part of the writing life; good, bad, or indifferent. The only remedy I can offer is to keep writing because — as I've said before — the only way a writer fails is not when they get rejected but when they stop writing.

And by keeping at it — trying to write each story better than the last one, and never giving up — you'll stay on the road to becoming perhaps not a great writer, but at least a better one: published, rejected, or not.

CHAPTER 34: VALENTINE'S DAY

I've said it before, but it bears repeating: writing is NOT easy — professionally for sure, but most of all psychologically. Any writer who sends their work out for consideration, as opposed to just sticking it in a drawer, is putting their emotional life on the line every time they mail the envelope or hit the SEND button. When a story is rejected, the writer has no one to blame but themselves. They can't point to the actors, the screenplay, or the special effects artists like a director can. They can't accuse the opening act, the acoustics, or the crowd like a musician can. When things go wrong for a writer it's just them, in the dark, with their mistakes.

That's why it's very important that you take care of yourself. Even though it's well nigh impossible, try to separate yourself from the work. Remind yourself that *you* didn't get rejected, the story did. Repeat the mantra that being a writer is a work in progress, that your next story will be better. Never forget that everyone — and this really is true — gets rejected. Try to hold your own hand, pat yourself on your own back and — most of all — keep working.

But there's a problem. Except for a few very rare exceptions, it's nearly impossible for you to perform that anatomical and emotional contortion of holding your own hand or patting yourself on the back ... or kissing your own cheek, bringing yourself a cup of unexpected but very needed tea, or telling yourself the magic words of "It's going to be okay" or "I believe in you."

This is where someone else comes in.

You won't find this listed in many books on writing, but I've come to realize that it's essential. Writing can be a very hard — and often lonely — life. But it doesn't have to be. Taking care of yourself is one facet of surviving as a writer, but finding someone who understands and cares about you and your work is essential. Some writers use friends, relatives, parents, or members of a support circle for a hand to hold, a shoulder to cry on, or a pal to laugh with.

Others are blessed with a partner who understands how hard being a writer can be, someone who knows the aches and pains as well as the joy of putting thoughts to paper. I'm lucky — very lucky — to have found that myself. I am fortunate beyond words to have a woman in my life who has given me what I've always wanted — someone to share writing and every other aspect of my life with:

I love you, Jill.

Sorry for the Hallmark moment, but I do have a point. As I said, I'm lucky. It took me a long time and just the right set of circumstances to get to the wonderful situation I'm in right now. Before—and this is also the case for many other people—I was involved with people who may have been caring and understanding, but who also simply didn't *get it*. What's worse is that many writers are involved with people who can't even provide the "caring and understanding" part of that, or who are uninterested in (if not resentful of or even hostile to) their partner's needs as a writer. I know this is a book on erotica, but I want to step beyond those boundaries and say that if anyone in your life isn't supportive, then you should dump them and move on. Writing is damned hard but being with someone who puts down your work, sabotages your craft, or makes writing harder than it already is not someone you should have in your life.

Beyond the obvious, though, or the supreme intimacy of sharing your bed as well as your writing with a partner, it can be very hard to notice when someone is no longer a help but has rather has become a hindrance. All too often when a writer finds a person who will even read, let alone critique, their work, they hang on to them like grim death, even when they are doing more harm than good. For example, here are some questions you should be asking when you get feedback from anyone, including a loving partner:

Are they speaking from prejudice? A good reader should be able to suspend their personal likes and dislikes and comment on only the story. If they rip the work—or you—apart because they personally don't like the sex, the setting, the characters, etc., without giving thoughtful feedback, then this is someone who doesn't deserve to see your work.

Are they jealous? Too often, an insecure reader will dig for fault when none is present because you have surprised or intimidated them with your abilities. This is not to say that all criticism should be viewed with paranoia, but when comments come with too much vitriol or they are making too much of small errors, then you might want to raise your eyebrows.

Are they making unfair comparisons? If your story was written for *Truckstop Transsexuals in Trouble*, you don't want a reader telling you that your style, characters, or setting is nowhere near the quality of Dickens, Hemingway, or Shakespeare.

Are they mixing you and your work? Back to *Truckstop Transsexuals*, you don't want comments like "Baby, I didn't know you were into that stuff," or "How often do you think about things like this?" or "I think you need therapy." You may very well need therapy, but you certainly don't need remarks like that.

Are the comments constructive? Get rid of—as fast as possible—anyone who does not say anything good about your work. If all you get are brutal criticisms or even just witty put-downs, then turn right around and insult the size, shape, or hygiene of their genitals. Okay, that might be a bit harsh, but a good reader will always give good with the bad, even if it's just that your font was pretty and you spelled most of the words correctly.

I could go on, but I hope I've made my point: the people in your life shouldn't make writing any harder than it already is. Find friends, pals, buddies or even lovers who know, understand, and sympathize with what being a writer is — and who, most importantly — will be there with a cup of tea, a kiss on the forehead, or even just a few kind and supportive words when baring your soul on the page gets just a little too cold, a bit too dark, or a touch too lonely.

You're a writer — and that's special and brave. You're worth it.

ASK A PROVOCATEUR: JUDE MASON

What makes a great erotic story?

Building sensual or sexual tension, and the ability to hold it there, will get my attention. There are writers who can make buying vegetables an erotic adventure. It's knowing how to titillate and not being afraid to draw it out that will make your reader squirm. Drawing them in, making them feel as if they're part of the story or identify with one of the characters will bring a reader back time and again. Erotica is escapism literature, so give that person somewhere sexy to escape to and you've got him/her.

* * * *

What would you tell someone who is just starting out as an erotica writer?

Read and write, a lot; repeat often and enjoy the ride. It's not as easy as many people seem to think, this sexy writing. Don't make that mistake. There's research and plotting, edits and re-writes, but if you stick to it, you'll succeed.

* * * *

What's a common mistake writers make when writing erotica?

I've found that, because it's just sexy writing, many new authors especially, don't think they have to do research They seem to think that if they come up with a cool story line and write it, the details don't matter. I suppose if you write only what is familiar and in the general locale where they live, this might be true. But, if they wander into a genre or have their characters travel to some foreign port or sci-fi other world, it's going to be an issue.

There is also the author who assumes that because they've come up with the most amazing of stories, it'll fit any publisher they send it to. Read the guides, folks, and follow them to a T. That's going to make you look 100% more professional and trust me, it'll be noticed.

* * * *

Multi-published Canadian author, Jude Mason, writes D/S, M/M, F/F, M/M, paranormal, fetish, sci-fi, romance and erotica, stretching the boundaries at every opportunity. Interested in finding out more, Google her name, you'll find her.

CHAPTER 35: THE BEST OF THE BEST OF THE BEST

Here's a quote that's very near and dear to my heart:

From the age of six I had a mania for drawing the shapes of things. When I was fifty I had published a universe of designs, but all I have done before the age of seventy is not worth bothering with. At seventy-five I'll have learned something of the pattern of nature, of animals, of plants, of trees, birds, fish and insects. When I am eighty you will see real progress. At ninety I shall have cut my way deeply into the mystery of life itself. At a hundred I shall be a marvelous artist. At a hundred and ten everything I create; a dot, a line, will jump to life as never before. To all of you who are going to live as long as I do, I promise to keep my word. I am writing this in my old age. I used to call myself Hokusai, but today I sign myself "The Old Man Mad About Drawing."

That was from Katsushika Hokusai, a Japanese painter of the Ukiyo-e school (1760-1849). Don't worry about not knowing him, because you do: he created the famous *Great Wave Off Kanagawa*, published in his "Thirty-six Views of Mount Fuji"—a print of which you've probably seen a thousand times.

Hokusai says it all: the work is what's really important, that he will always continue to grow and progress as an artist, and that who he is will always remain less than what he creates.

Writing is like art. We struggle to put our thoughts and intimate fantasies down just so, and then we send them out into an often harsh and uncaring world, hoping that someone out there will pat us on the head, give us a few coins, and tell us we did a good job.

What with this emotionally chaotic environment a little success can push just about anyone into feeling overly superior. Being kicked and punched by the trials and tribulations of the writing life makes just about anyone desperate to feel good about themselves, even if it means losing perspective or looking down on other writers. Arrogance becomes an emotional survival tool, a way of convincing themselves they deserve to be patted on the noggin a few more times than anyone else, paid more coins, and told they are beyond brilliant, extremely special.

It's very easy to spot someone afflicted with this. Since their superiority constantly needs to be buttressed, they measure and weigh the accomplishments and merits of other writers to decide if they are better—and so should be humbled—or worse—and so should be the source of worship or admiration. In writers, this can come off as someone who thinks they deserve better in everything than anyone else: pay, attention, consideration, etc. In editors, this appears as rudeness, terseness, or an unwillingness to treat contributors as anything but a resource to be exploited.

Now my house has more than a few windows, and I have more than enough stones, so I say all this with a bowed head: I am not exactly without this sin. But I do think that trying to treat those around you as equals should be the goal of every human on this planet, let alone folks with literary aspirations. Sometimes we might fail, but even trying as best we can — or at least owning the emotion when it gets to be too much — is better than embracing an illusion of superiority.

What this has to do with erotica writing has a lot to do with marketing. As I wrote back in "Peddling Your Ass," arrogance can be a serious roadblock for a writer. It is an illusion — and a pervasive one — that good work will always win out. This is true to a certain extent, but there are a lot of factors that can step in the way of reading a great story and actually buying it. Part of that is the relationship that exists between writers and publishers or editors. A writer who honestly believes they are God's gift to mankind might be able to convince a few people, but after a point their stories will be more received with a wince than a smile: no matter how good a writer they are, their demands are just not worth it.

For editors and publishers, arrogance shows when more and more authors simply don't want to deal with them. After a point, they might find themselves with a shallower and shallower pool of talent from which to pick their stories — and as more authors get burned by their attitude and the word spreads, they might also find that the word has spread to more influential folks, like publishers.

Not to take away from the spiritual goodness of being kind to others, acting superior is also simply a bad career move. This is a very tiny community, with a lot of people moving around. Playing God might be fun for a few years, but all it takes is stepping on a few too many toes — especially toes that belong on the feet of someone who might suddenly be able to help you in a big way some day — making arrogance a foolish role to play.

I am not a Christian (despite my pseudonym) but they have a great way of saying it, one that should be tacked in front of everyone's forehead: "Do onto others as you would have them do unto you." It might not be as elegant and passionate as my Hokusai quote, but it's still a maxim we should all strive to live by — professionally as well as personally.

CHAPTER 36: TOOTING

There are a lot of myths about being a writer: fame, fortune, tweed coats with leather patches, million-dollar advances, movie deals, publisher-sponsored book tours and so forth. Not that there aren't a few instances of these things being true, but for their rarity, they might as well be right up there with unicorns and trolls under bridges.

In other words, the writer who only depends on only on his or her publisher for publicity is going to find their work quickly forgotten.

Certainly some publishers are very good about heralding their books, but that still doesn't mean they're going to do all the work. It all comes down to numbers: even a great publisher has a lot of books to sell: they simply don't have time or resources to publicize each and every one. Most of the time you're lucky if the publisher sends out a dozen or so review copies or galleys, let alone does the legwork and makes the calls to drum up interest. Getting your book published, in other words, is just part of the battle: you have to do even more work to get your work noticed.

There is a fine line in publicity, one that's way too easy to cross: one side is humility and invisibility, and on the other is hyperbole and arrogance. The trick, obviously, is to try and put you and your work somewhere between the two. I wish I could say I'm good at this, but to be honest I have the same problem other writers have with publicity: not knowing whether I've become one or the other until it's almost too late.

Two classic mainstays of publicity are press releases and author interviews. Sure, they might be old school but the ideas hold even into this new age. Press releases are simple in concept, but take some skill to create effectively. They should be short, a page to a page in a half, be relevant to various media outlets, and give all the info the media outlets need to write up something about your book.

For interviews, you can create your own—which works quite often— or ask regular interviewer to do one and send it out with your press stuff. The trick with interviews, or any publicity for that matter, is to make then *interesting* so that venues will use them. Just chatting about your book isn't usually enough, so try to make them witty, provocative, thought provoking, and so forth. Like with press releases this can take a bit of practice to don't give up if your first attempts are a bit rough around the edges.

Linking up with another writer is a great idea as it not only adds to your own exposure but that way you can split the work of getting your interview or such out there. This is why making good net connections is very important since when they scratch your back you can then scratch … well, you get it. This is why connections and friendships are essential to getting the word out about your book. More on this later when I get to blogging and such.

Readings used to be a mainstay of book publicity but, what with the Internet and all, they have pretty much fallen by the wayside. Do the math: a reading takes hours—both the reading itself as well as the grinding work of getting it set up and getting the word out—but if you sit at home and send out press releases and interviews and the like you can reach ten times that number while still in your bathrobe. Besides, bookstores used to be where books were sold—but not anymore. Now books are mostly sold through online stores, so it makes much more sense to direct your publicity in that direction.

A very import rule of thumb for publicity is, like with bookstore readings, bang for your buck: if you are spending too much time talking about your writing, instead of writing, then it's time to rethink how you're handling things.

This is why I'm such a curmudgeon when it comes to the social networking flavor-of-the-month. Sure, pay attention to how things might be changing as well as new opportunities but if you get seduced by everything that comes up then you'll just be wasting your time. Twitter is a perfect example of this. Even though lots of people swear by it, I still think that it takes far too much time to maintain a good twitter feed. Fine if you're a professional twitter-er but if you have a life, or, importantly, writing to do, then it just gets in the way.

As for what to say and how to avoid sounding like a self-important jerk, take a good look at what you've accomplished and try and present it realistically, though attractive enough for a reviewer to pick up. Try and get some nice juicy blurbs from other writers, especially those you recognize and respect—or who sell books. In your press release, mention and quote any reviews you may have gotten, though be careful of getting permission—some don't care, but others are very prickly about such things. Avoid hyperbole in describing yourself or your accomplishments. This might work in getting your name out there, but can cause problems when other writers, editors and publishers get annoyed at you calling yourself "the greatest living American writer," though if a lot of other, neutral folks have called you that, then go for it. Also, try and keep your announcements down to a dull roar or set up an email list so people at least know that your messages will be a regular and informative newsletter and not just an "I'm fantastic" email that arrives in their in-boxes every few months, unsolicited.

A word about mailing lists: there are several companies that provide them so you don't have to worry that your ISP will think you're spamming.

Another cold hard fact about publicity is that it usually only works for books. Short stories in anthologies, magazines, and Web sites simply aren't impressive enough to warrant a press release. The best you can do for shorts in magazines, Web site and anthologies is volunteer yourself for readings and offer possible reviewers or interviewers for the editor.

Doing publicity always reminds me of the joke: a man is constantly entreating God to let him win the lottery. Finally, fed up, God responds, "Meet me half-way: buy a ticket." In others words, the reality of writing is that success comes to those who try, try again, try some more, and— more than anything—keep trying. The work of making your book a success doesn't stop when you finish writing it. In fact, that's often just half the battle. The rewards, luckily, are more than worth it, especially when you get your first good reviews or people actually start to know your name.

CHAPTER 37: SHUT UP!

You've seen them everywhere on the web: Amazon, Netflix, the Internet Movie Database, and too many more to name. They are usually called different things depending on the site, but each and every one boils down the same thing: the chance for some ignorant idiot to express his or her American Right of Free Speech. *Reader Reviews, Featured Member Reviews,* or *Customer Reviews,* call them what you will but I always think—or even say—the same thing when I see them:

Shut Up!

I've said it before and I'll say it again, creating anything is damned hard work. Movies, books, plays, music, painting—anything. It takes determination, lots of failures, facing a lot of personal demons, and a helluva lot of other icky stuff just to make something out of nothing, let alone send it out there into the world. What needlessly makes it harder is when that work is splattered by some unenlightened pinhead that feels that because they can say something nasty, they should.

Sour grapes? You betcha. But believe it or not, this isn't about reviews for anything I've written. Instead, this rant is about the reviews I've seen for what I thought where thoroughly excellent movies, books or what have you—demeaned if not ruined by droolers who can't wait to show off their smarts by trashing something that took an author, painter, musician or movie crew years to create. Oh, yes, I've heard it all before: the sacredness of Free Speech, the Web as "the great equalizer," the chance for the little guy to be heard. I'm all for intelligent discussions and thoughtful criticism but if you can't be intelligent, can't manage thoughtful, then keep your gob shut.

What does this have to do with writing? Well, aside from perhaps putting a dollop of empathy in those of you out there that like to post bad reader reviews, this is also about how to give good criticism.

Too often writers work in the dark, meaning they have absolutely no idea if their work is any good. They show it to mothers, fathers, boyfriends, girlfriends and so forth who obviously are not going to say anything but "fantastic, honey!" The only other option is to find a writer's group, a bunch of folks who share the same goal: to write as well as they can. The problem is that groups too often catch the same pitiful disease that infects Reader's Review posters. Straight up insults or what are thought to be "witty" jokes fly, personal tastes get in the way, jealousy clouds respect, old hands turn into old crows, and people get hurt for no good reason.

Rule of Thumb for Giving Good Criticism #1: Don't give criticism that you wouldn't like to get. Think before telling or writing anything about another writer. Put yourself in their shoes, especially if it's someone just starting out. Would you like to hear that your story sucked? Of course not. So don't say it.

Rule of Thumb for Giving Good Criticism #2: Don't be funny. Make jokes on your own time, not at the expense of someone else. Criticism is not your stage; it's talking about someone else's. If you want applause, get up there on the stage yourself. Otherwise, see the title of this column.

Rule of Thumb for Giving Good Criticism #3: Give as well as take. Never give a completely bad review of someone else's work. A lot of things go into a story: plot, characterizations, dialogue, descriptions, pacing — it can't all be bad. I've very often hated a film but loved the soundtrack, one special actor, the dialogue in one scene, whatever. Leave the author something that they did well, even if it was just that the paper was clean.

Rule of Thumb for Giving Good Criticism #4: This story wasn't written for you. The fact that the story didn't turn you on is your problem, not the author's. I can't say this enough. If you hate westerns but you have to critique someone's western story, don't say you hate westerns — or do I really have to be that obvious?

Rule of Thumb for Giving Good Criticism #5: Leave your baggage at home. If you don't like the politics in a story, then shut up. If you don't enjoy a certain kind of food mentioned in a story, then shut up. If you don't like a kind of sex in a story, then shut up. If you don't like ... you get the point.

Rule of Thumb for Giving Good Criticism #6: Be specific. No, not down to word and sentence, but rather avoid saying things like the plot was "bad," or "dumb," or "predictable." Rather, give useful information: "There was too much foreshadowing, especially on page two. I could see the ending coming from then on."

I could go on, but I hope I've made my point. If I could sum all this up into a rather long fortune cookie, it would be to try and remember that it's easier to criticize than create, but more important to create than criticize — or at least help create, rather than harm.

ASK A PROVOCATEUR: SHANNA GERMAIN

What makes a great erotic story?

For me, great erotic stories arouse both my body and my brain. I want to come to know complex, REAL characters, to be turned on by and with them, to learn their own individual sexual triggers and needs, to take a journey through their desire and lust. The best stories are the ones that surprise me, that take away my breath with a moment of discovery. I'm not great with recipes, but I'd say something along the lines of:

+ one or two (or more) complex, real characters;
+ one moment of discovery or surprise,
+ a few good-size portions of sexuality and sensuality,
+ a heaping spoonful of fine writing or fantastic voice,
+ a dash of delight,
+ and a pinch of ass.

* * * *

What would you tell someone who is just starting out as an erotica writer?

Sit in your room and say all the "naughty" words aloud to yourself. Say *cock* and *clit* and *cunt* over and over until you're not nervous about it anymore (And if you weren't nervous in the first place, say them over and over anyway, until the words become ripe fruits, poems, love letters in your mouth). Then write your ass off. You're going to suck for the first year. Maybe two. So get used to it. And when you're ready to hear how much you suck so that you can get better, find a really, really great critique group. And don't give up.

* * * *

What's a common mistake writers make when writing erotica?

Getting so steeped in the clichés of porn and bad movies that they don't create real people or real sex. If you're writing about boob size or waist size or dick size, stop right there. Reconsider. Think of the people you've fucked, the people you've loved, the people you've lusted after. What turned you on? The way their eyes looked behind the lenses of the reading glasses they always wore to bed? That mousy squeak they made after you hooked nipple clamps on? The taste of their skin mid-fuck?

Get specific. Get real. Real people are messy and fumbling and imperfect; so is real sex. Everyone is beautiful and sexy and full of lust. Everyone. Always. Tell me about them.

* * * *

Shanna Germain loves writing about things that go bump in the night; thus her two favorite genres are horror and erotica. Her work has appeared in places like *Absinthe Literary Review, Best American Erotica, Best Gay Bondage Erotica, Best Gay Romance, Best Lesbian Erotica, Best Lesbian Romance, Blood Fruit: Queer Horror* and Bitten: *Dark Erotic Stories.*

CHAPTER 38: EBOOK, EPUBLISHER, EFUN

"My name is Chris and I ... until recently ... used to be a printed book addict."

Yes, dear readers, I had it bad: bookstores used to suck me in, tearing the money out of my wallet for, at first, a single paperback, but then whole boxes and then entire bookcases of reading materials.

My bedroom walls were covered by bookshelves of paperbacks, my coffee table's legs bowed under the weight of picture books, my toilet tank cracked from the weight of stacked hardbacks, and my nightstand always had a perilous pre-topple of trade paperbacks. Professionally, I looked at printed books as the one-and-only, and glowered at those who'd gone the ebook route.

I said *until recently* because a few years ago, that changed. This is the story of how I went from being a printed book junkie to an ebook booster.

Part of it was simple pragmatism: publisher after publisher after publisher has simply closed up shop — and the few that remain have cut their buying dramatically. No one likes to say it out loud, but it's commonly understood that if you're a writer who insists on publishing exclusively in print ... well, it must feel very much like being a master calligrapher looking for work after Gutenberg changed the world with moveable type.

The other part is when I looked around at my bedroom walls, my coffee table, my bathroom, my bedroom, my kitchen, and then my basement — and realized with a chill that while, yes, it's still very nice to hold a book in your hand, relish the crispness of the paper, feel the weight of it, breath the smell of it, print books are actually tremendously wasteful ... and not good for writers.

Think of it this way: your book comes out from a traditional printed-book publisher. That's fine. That's dandy. But if they only printed a few thousand — if you're lucky — copies, then that's all there is. Ever. Unless it sells well enough to go into a second printing, which happens, but it's not common. Once those are gone, for whatever reason, your work is nothing but a memory — and then after you and the few people who read your book are gone it's nothing but ... well, nothing.

Ebooks have their flaws, but once an ebook is published, it can stay accessible for as long as there's an Internet: days, weeks, centuries, eons even. There's virtually no cost to send out a single copy or a million.

Each ebook you write can sit out there forever, waiting patiently to be discovered and enjoyed.

Because printed-book publishers basically have to bet on an author's popularity, there's a large amount of pressure on a writer to perform. If you don't sell enough copies, you simply aren't worth their time or energy to publish again. If an ebook doesn't sell, it might not be ideal, but it isn't a disaster for the author or the publisher.

The same is true for bookstores. If an author doesn't sell, they don't re-order their books—and if they don't re-order books, the publisher starts to question not just that particular author but maybe even that entire genre.

Even ecologically printed books are bad: trees for paper, energy for printing and shipping, energy for those who recycle them or landfills for those who stupidly won't. Honestly, do you want to see Al Gore cry?

A great side effect of the ebook revolution is that almost anyone can become a publisher, even writers themselves. Yes, it's possible that the world will become supersaturated with publishers to a point where writers won't be able to get themselves heard above the noise of them all. But it also means that if you write it, more than likely someone will publish it.

So what makes a good ebook publisher? It really depends on what you're looking for: a big one so you'll have name recognition by proxy or a smaller and *hungrier* house where every book is special because you're one of dozens and not thousands? Do you want to work with a publisher who only handles erotica or with one who puts out a wide range of books? Do you want someone who will either print your work as an ebook as well as a printed one, or would you be fine with just a digital edition? Only you know what will suit you best. Isn't it nice to have options?

By the way, just in case some of you haven't heard, print isn't likely to die. Instead, it will probably become an option called "Print on Demand" where a hardcopy will be printed, well, *on demand* and shipped out to you. The technology is already here.

The best thing, though, about the ebook revolution, which I'll be writing about more, is the flexibility it gives to writers. For every print publisher closing its doors, a new crop of ebook publishers springs up, offering a whole new world for writers to explore. There are options today that have never existed, ever. Think of today not as the fading of traditional print publishers but instead an explosion of possibilities and options. If you don't like one publisher there are dozens—if not hundreds—of others out there who might think you're the best writer who ever lived, or at least treat you really well.

Yes, I miss the smell of books, the feel of books, even the taste of books, but then I fire up my Mac, or flick my finger across the screen of my iPhone, and there are books after books after books after books, from

Homer to Steinbeck to Hugo to Verne, to Dickens to virtual unknowns like this M. Christian guy

And that is truly, staggeringly, awesome.

CHAPTER 39: ESTILL EMORE EBOOK EFUN

… in our last installment, Professor Ghostly and the Wildly Gesticulating Windup Sparrows from Tomorrow's Spain were facing off against the Whimpering Menace of the Cutout Dolls while the Perpetually Perky Percy Pureheart and the Men from Boy's Own Adventure, Ltd., raced against time to get the Pearl of Solvency back to the Citadel of Missing Keys and end of the reign of the Tuneless Dogs once and for all …

Ooops—sorry: wrong story. What was I talking about? Oh, yes: ebooks. Though I have to admit the story of Professor Ghostly does sound kind of interesting ….

Anyway, I mentioned in my last installment that choosing a publisher—or more than one, which I'll get to in a sec—is very subjective thing. What you like, or want, in an ebook publisher might not be what someone else wants. So just what criteria should you use in selecting the ebook publisher for you?

Here's a quick—and by no means complete—rundown of some of the things to consider when choosing an ebook publisher.

Size is an important consideration. Many writers like working with a house that has a large—if not huge—stock of titles. They feel that such publishers likely have a lot of experience as well as resources. Maybe that's true, but maybe it isn't. Don't be quick to dismiss a smaller house; with them, you might be important, rather than just one of a thousand. As a result, they may have more of a stake in your success.

Another factor to keep in mind is how they handle your genre of choice: do they handle multiple genres, one of which is erotica? This diversity is good because it means you can probably branch out if you want to without having to switch publishers. But if they specialize in erotica, is also means they would more than likely act as a landmark for the genre, so you could have a bigger audience with them.

Most publishers understand, if not support, a writer working with more than one publisher. They understand that if you succeed with another publisher, your popularity will carry over to them. But some publishers prefer to have a writer be theirs alone. They like the idea of building a brand. The choice is yours but frankly, I'd suggest a really hefty payment for this kind of ownership because it means you won't be able to expand your writing out to anyone else.

Alas, advances have vanished—though a few rare publishers offer small amounts—so percentage of sales is the new thing. I wish I could offer a concrete *good* or *bad* breakdown, but it really depends on your situation and what you might also want out of a publisher. Being happy and feeling warm and cozy with your publisher may very well be more precious to you than a check.

Looks may also be an important consideration: does your publisher create attractive packages, or is this not important to you? Some feel that covers are also going the way of the dinosaur and that content will again prove to be king, but other people feel that, like a good meal, the reading experience begins with the eyes. Again, this is up to you.

What content and copy editing does your publisher offer? Some work very hard to make a book as clean as possible while others pass that work off to the writers. As a notoriously sloppy writer, I like a publisher that has good copyeditors and struggles to make my work sound like English, but if you're a master of the language, that may not be as important to you.

Publicity, as most of us know all too well, is key these days. One might even call it essential. So how your publisher spreads the word about you and your book may be important to you: do you want them to help you out with getting your work out there, or is that something you feel you can do better yourself?

Here's an important one: is the publisher you're thinking of a good fit for you? Can you see yourself being the author of one of their titles? Many people see who they work with as a symbol of their success, while others see a publisher as simply a means of getting their work out there while they work on their own image as a writer.

Okay … that should give you a bit to think about. Keep in mind that, aside from issues such as "Is your publisher honest?" and "will your publisher pay you what you're due?" — which you can usually discover by asking other writers and doing a bit of research — the rest is really just a matter of personal preference. And it's just one of the big changes that the switch from book to ebook has brought.

Now if you'll excuse me, I have to get back to Professor Ghostly, and find out what publisher I'd like to work with to get him and his adventures out into the world ….

CHAPTER 40: TO BLOG OR NOT TO BLOG

Should you blog? Yes.

What, you want reasons? (sigh.) Okay, here are a few good reasons why you should immediately – or close to immediately – start your own blog and what you should put in it.

First of all, as I've said, everything's changed, especially in the writing world. Understand that these days, in this new world, anyone can be a writer, which is the good news as well as the bad news.

While publicity and exposure have never been things a writer could ignore, or did so at their peril, they've now become absolutely essential. You have to find some way – any way – of standing out from a growing throng of people who are also yelling at the top of their literary lungs for the attention of editors, publishers, or even readers.

Blogging is a great way to do just that: it's free, easy, fun, and a good way to show off your work and build an audience. Frankly, there isn't a reason not to blog, aside from the seduction of spending too much time on it, thereby keeping you from what's really important, which is your fiction writing.

Two things to think about before you start:

1) Pick a platform. There are plenty of options, and more every day, so take some time and do some research. Since most blog sites are free, and frankly there is no reason to pay for one, go ahead and try a few out: you don't have to keep any you don't like. Important questions to ask yourself as you play include how what options you have, how customizable it is, and how it looks. Ease of use is essential: believe me, you don't want a blog that's so hard to use it keeps you from adding to it. Ideally a blog should be not only interesting for your readers but comfortable for you to maintain.

2) You have to decide what your blog's about. It's tempting to make it a personal thing, a site to show off your writing. Although that approach is fine and good, those types of blogs can (at best) sometimes be a bit dull or, at worst, make a writer feel obligated to constantly post new content. I recommend either:

> + a blog mixed with a hobby other than your writing, or
> + two separate sites: one for your writing that you don't update a lot and one you post a lot of fun stuff to.

Say, for instance, that you like food. Then do a sex and food blog that mixes your work with food-related stuff. (Donna George Storey does this well with her *Sex, Food, and Writing* blog.) Or you could do sex and movies, sex and travel, sex and ... well, it's really up to you. Just do what you feel comfortable doing because that's the only way you'll continue to blog.

Personal experience time! I'm not an expert, but I've had a lot of fun with my own blogs — and they seem to be going fairly well. I've created three separate blogs:

M. Christian (www.mchristian.com) is a site where I post my writing stuff (reviews, stories, essays like the one you're reading right now, book announcements, and such).

Meine Kleine Fabrik (meinekleinefabrik.blogspot.com) is the site my brother and I started to share the fun and weird stuff we've collected over the years or just stumbled across.

Frequently Felt (frequentlyfelt.blogspot.com) is where I post funny and strange sex stuff as well as work by writers who I've either contacted or who have sent me great things to post (and you can do the same — just write me).

I recommend posting at least once a day, and consistently; people forget very quickly about dead or slow sites. You have to keep things flowing to keep people interested and reading. Once a day works for me, as I can post to all three blogs in about half an hour, which leaves me a lot of time to work on my fiction writing. I also cheat a bit in that I rarely write fresh content for my blogs, preferring to repost older material instead of spending precious time writing new stuff. I'm fortunate to have archives bursting with material, but I realize not everybody will be in a similar position. Basically, do what you can to prevent the blog from sucking time away from your "real" writing!

There are lots of sites out there with hints and techniques for running a successful blog, so I won't go into much detail about that topic here (besides, as I said, it's all new and changing anyway). Here's a quick rundown of things to remember, though, when you're blogging.

One of the biggest, and most confusing, things about running a blog is posting content that isn't your own. Technically, and legally, you should always get permission from the original source, but that's too often a huge headache and/or impossible. This is where what you should do (legally) and what most people go (realistically) part ways. Since I always try to be a law-abiding citizen ... stop laughing ... I must advise you to follow established procedure. There's lots of sites out there that can help you with your copyright questions. Check out the U.S. Copyright Office's list of resource links for more information. I feel Creative Commons offers some of the best (and simplest) solutions and resources to make this topic less confusing.

Beyond the fun of figuring out what's legal, a common mistake bloggers make is not putting an email address on their site(s). Yes you'll get spammed (we all do) but what's worse: spam or not hearing from some editor, publisher, or reader? I've tried to reach out to many writers only to find no way of reaching them on their site – and so they've lost an opportunity. These days, writers can't afford to lose any possible gig or connection.

It's also important to play with gadgets and gizmos. Blogger has all kinds of cool modules you can add to your site: video clips, sound clips, RSS readers, you name it. People expect multimedia these days — pages and pages of text is a kiss of death for blogs.

Checking out other blogs and sites is essential. There's nothing wrong with learning from other's successes and doing to your own site what they've done to theirs. As long as your content is different, there is no harm done. And the aforementioned gadgets and modules make it very easy to add or subtract features. Just experiment and see what works, or doesn't, for you.

I could go on, but this should at least give you a start. Think about what you want to do with your blog, settle on a focus you can play with for a long time, and then set it up. Once it's done and you feel good about sticking with it, then you can begin to reach out. Again, more on that very soon.

But in the meantime always remember that blogs are like writing and life itself: if it's not fun, if you're not enjoying yourself, then you're doing something wrong. So have yourself a blast with this great exposure and publicity tool – and blog away!

* * * *

Exercises:

1. Before you create one, try looking at various blogs and making a personal survey of what you like, or don't, about them. Importantly, though, look at the site as a reader and not as another writer: far too many sites are slick and professional but turn off readers who might want more personal stuff about their favorite authors. Also pay attention to what blogging tools they might be using. If they are doing something, there's no reason you can't as well.

2. Make some lists of what kinds of things your blog can be about— aside from yourself. Are you into history? Movies? Food? Travel? Weird Stuff? Just, please, no cats. Okay, if you want cats then do cats— don't let me stop you. Just keep in mind that your goal is to be comfy running a blog for quite a while so be honest with yourself about what you can maintain.

3. Create a blog. Go on, it won't bite. If it sucks—and it may just do that—then you can always change it. Play with the formatting, the style, the colors, the interface. You don't have to share it with anyone, just practice with the set-up and the functions. If you're nervous about "wasting" posts on an early site … don't. There's no reason why you can't just repost them when the site officially launches.

CHAPTER 41: MEETING PEOPLE, MAKING FRIENDS

So now you have a blog. What do you do now?

Your immediate instinct might be to start trumpeting the horns and shouting from the rooftops: I have a blog! But I advise restraint. For one thing people, coming to your little piece of cyberspace promotion or other fun stuff will find almost nothing there, and two, you should get comfortable running your blog before trying to get people to look it. Don't worry about your cool stuff possibly vanishing into the archives, because when you get your audience, lots of people will explore all your nooks and crannies.

So a weaning period is recommended. How long naturally depends on you and your dedication. After you've gotten comfortable with the style and maintenance of your blog, then it's time to start telling folks about it. One of the easiest ways is to add a link to your site in the footer of your emails, the same with any forum posts you might do. Friends, of course, should be told when you have your blog up and running, plus any writer circles you might run in.

But one of the best ways is to reach out to sites similar to yours. Offer a link exchange, which means you put a link to them on your site and they do the same to yours. You can do this easily by sending out emails with the offer — which is another reason why you should always put your email address on your site, so people can reach out to you, too. A nice gesture, by the way, is to publicly thank people who agree to reciprocal linking. Yes, that means thanking them on your blog, and linking to their site when you mention them.

That's how you make friends, which is what this is all about. Being a writer is all too often a thankless if not brutal way of life: no money, little respect, not much recognition, lots of psychological bruising if not outright scarring — so the least we can do is try to be nice to one another, to show a little support and kindness to fellow writers, and most of all, to yourself.

The huge swell of writers, the ongoing collapse — or at best, restructuring — of traditional publishing, and the general economic turmoil have made many people insecure, arrogant, and pointlessly competitive, making a difficult situation needlessly worse. So, writers and bloggers, please try and be part of a solution and not just the problem. Be kinder and more courteous than the majority of self-absorbed publicity machines out there. Set an example.

Your blog, believe it or not, can help. Work to make it part of a community and not just a platform for self-aggrandizing. Reach out to people not just for links and traffic numbers but to make real connections: it's not just a friendly thing to do but connections, especially these days, are tremendously important—no one can afford to let any opportunity pass them by.

And try to offer help to people who need it. My Frequently Felt blog is an example: I've opened it up to all kinds of people deserving of attention—artists, writers, you name it. While I do post my own stuff there, I usually reserve most of my promo stuff for my pro site at mchristian.com. I've made some good connections through this site, but more importantly I've made friends—really good friends—that have made the hard life of being a writer much easier, and whom I sincerely hope I've helped in return.

You can also help make the blogosphere a better place by **not** doing something. Stop giving exposure to people who don't need it. It's very easy to try and curry favor by linking to celebrity writers, hoping for some attention in return. I'm not immune: I used to do the same thing myself. But then I began to get really frustrated: why should I give attention to someone who ignores my friendly emails, who is clearly playing a much more aggressive game of sucking up to even bigger names, and who never seems to do anything but rave about their own successes? What I guess I'm saying is reward kindness, support, and understanding—not just fame—when you're working on your own community.

One of the simplest things you can do to build your blog is to be responsive: post comments on other people's blog posts and email them when you mention them in your own. If someone writes you—for any reason (well, aside from spam)—write them back, even if it's just a simple "thanks but no thanks." If someone comments on your blog, thank them with an email or another comment. It makes me angry to hear other writers talk about deleting emails when their inbox gets too full—or even, in weird cases, feeling a sense of superiority in not answering messages. Opportunities are few and far between, and can come from very unusual directions: today's friendly comment might be tomorrow's friend, and then a publishing deal sometime down the road. The reverse is true: will you reach out to people with your new, big, book project who don't answer your messages, who ignore everyone but themselves, or will you invite your friends, or at least people who treat you with simple respect?

Hopefully this will get you thinking about your blog, your site, and where you want to go with it.

ASK A PROVOCATEUR: THOMAS S. ROCHE

What makes a great erotic story?

I think there's no one answer to that, as far as sexuality goes. There are two kind of different things going on with erotic storytelling; there's the fantasy, and there's the story. The two interact, but they're not the same thing, exactly, or not always. There's no one set of criteria that makes a fantasy erotic—it's individual to readers, more than writers. But there are things that make for great storytelling, and so a truly great erotic story will also be a great story, period. I've read terribly written stories that are still hot, but that doesn't make them professional, and it doesn't make them great.

* * * *

What would you tell someone who is just starting out as an erotica writer?

Do it because you love doing it, not because you want to make money.

If you can, find a small number of readers who get off on your stories, and trust their opinions. If you do want to make any money, write novels, nonfiction, or both. You can learn to write by writing short stories or articles, but if you don't move on to longer works, your career will be limited, unless you're Borges or Harlan Ellison.

* * * *

What's a common mistake writers make when writing erotica?

There are a lot of them. They send out mediocre work. They don't edit and rewrite enough. Or they edit and rewrite too much. They linger on stories that just aren't that good, which means they're not creating new work. They don't learn about the business. They don't learn contract law. They don't learn grammar; they don't learn copyediting.

They listen to editors who hate any kind of innovation. They don't think big. They don't try to hold themselves up to the standard of great writers who make an overall impact on culture, rather than the standard of the workaday not-that-good writers they're competing with.

They don't experiment; they don't adventure. They don't go out and live life and bring back new stories to tell.

Also, they stop reading. They read a few books and they think they're "educated" on writing. If you take writing seriously, read constantly. I am convinced that many of my fellow writers don't read that much.

* * * *

Thomas S. Roche is the author of hundreds of published short stories in the genres of erotica, fantasy, horror and crime. He has edited three volumes of the *Noirotica* anthology of erotic crime-noir and co-edited four books of fantasy and horror stories. His short story collections include *Dark Matter, His and Hers*, the latter two co-written with Alison Tyler.

CHAPTER 42: THINKING BEYOND SEX

Say you've written an erotica book. What's more, it's a quality erotica book, which is to say that it isn't just about positions, sensations, steamy looks, and lingerie. It has an engaging setting, multidimensional characters, and a plot. It's well written and seeks to do more than turn the reader on. Hurray, and congratulations! I've said it before, but it certainly bears repeating: this is an incredible feat. There are very few people in this world that could have done what you've done. Take a moment to luxuriate in your success.

Done luxuriating? Good. Now you've sent your book out and congratulations (part two), you've managed to find a publisher for your novel—this is no mean feat, especially these days. So now you've written a book, you've sold a book, and soon it's going to be for sale.

Now is the time you must do something very important, and it may surprise you, given the genre in which your book is written.

Don't. Think. About. Sex.

I know, I know—a bit weird, right? After all, you've written an erotica book. So it seems more than natural that you'd want to reach out to sexy, kinky, smutty, erotica venues—and well, you should. But after you do that, you should really try and reach out to places a bit more … tangential.

Let me explain: erotica is a fine and dandy genre (I'm not disparaging it), but it's also a bit limiting. In erotica, your book is one of dozens, and every last one of them is clamoring to be the center of attention. Sure, yours is different—for whatever reason—but in the erotica world, your book is common first, and special second.

Let's say, for example, that your book is about a soldier during World War II. So why aren't you thinking about your book being a World War II book? Sure, you know you wrote it as erotica, and that's certainly essential to the book's allure, but its more than that, see? Try reaching out to soldier sites and World War II sites (and authors, forums, and such). Sure, there's a damn good chance your emails and announcements will be ignored, but if someone does respond then your book will really stand out: a World War II book—but an EROTICA one. Wow! Unique! Different!

In fact, I'll bet if you really looked at your book, you could find several places to branch off. Is it a love story? Then it could be romance. Is there a mystery involved? Then it could be—well, you get the idea.

Here's an important detail. You should absolutely tweak your announcements in a way to reach these different audiences. Instead of "erotic" and "explicit," try "sensual" and "stirring"—play up your book's connection to their world: *a sensual tale of a love and intimacy set in the latter days of World War II* ... that kind of thing.

Yeah, I know that sounds like another bit of Madison Avenue trickery, but keep in mind that for many people, the whole idea of a book with any kind of sexual content is a brain turn-off. You have to get them to see your book more broadly—as a bona fide story, rather than merely a sexual tale. The only way to do that sometimes is to squeak it in under their radar. No, I'm not saying you should lie, but what I am saying is this: why get the door shut in your face before you've even had a chance to say one word about your cherished novel?

Thinking of yourself as an erotica writer and your work as nothing but erotica will limit you as well as your publicity opportunities. Look beyond that simple label, and so will readers. You know your book is more than *Dick In Jane*; you know there's something special about it—so why not use that uniqueness to open a whole new world for both you and your works? Not only will this outlook give you a possible new audience, but you'd be shocked by the number of connections that also could emerge from stepping into other genres and interests. Someone who never would have dreamed of reading so-called smut suddenly has their eyes opened—by you, with your wonderful book.

So try and use the imagination you've developed in your writing to expand more than just your storytelling: try expanding on other possible places for exposure—and other possible places for you to grow and develop as a writer.

CHAPTER 43: SELLING BOOKS

Every author wants their books to sell ... right? Listen long enough, and you'll get a bookstore (remember those?) full of theories about what can push a title up the lists from few to many to bestseller and maybe even beyond: reviews, podcasts, blog tours, t-shirts, coffee mugs, MySpace, Facebook, Twitter, contests, eBay, interviews, tattoos, action figures ... you name it.

I'll go into some of those ideas—the good, the bad, and the just plain nuts—soon enough but in the meantime, I want to talk about what I consider the most important thing every writer needs to do when it comes time to put their book out into the world.

Well, actually, what they should do *before* it's time to put their book out into the world—in fact, after they've just finished writing it.

The problem, you see, is that far too often authors—and even some publishers—think in terms of a single book, and having one book be the end-all, be-all bestseller of all time, the book that launches a fantastic career. The hard truth, though, is that while that does happen, it's so rare that it might as well as not happen. Let me rephrase that: the odds are decidedly against your first book (or any other writer's) leaping off the shelves. Nor is it likely to put lots of cash in your pocket.

So what's the reality? When you look at the careers of successful (for now I'm going to ignore the fact that success is a very, very subjective term) writers, you'll find that they worked their way up those book lists one book at a time. But don't think in terms of *this book made a little money, the next one made a little bit more* and then—finally—*KA-CHING!* Nope. Mostly what happens is that one book might do well, the next not so much, the one after that a bit better, the following one badly, then—if they're lucky—a bestseller ... very much up and down, up and down.

And what ensues when that one bestseller does happen? Not only does that one book will sell well, but all those people who enjoyed it will also, very often, hunt down that author's other books as well. Suddenly books that didn't sell two copies at publication now leap off the shelves as readers hungrily consume their newly discovered favorite.

But this only happens with authors who have books in their inventory. See where this is going? If you only have one book, you're spending a lot of time pushing your way up the lists. If it does manage to sell, and sell well, then your readers have only that book to read. If you have a stock of several books, however, your readers will be able to get into your entire stock of works ... going from casual readers to loyal fans.   If that's not enough of a motivation, then keep in mind that sometimes success can come from totally unexpected directions. Remember I mentioned that sometimes a book just doesn't sell, or doesn't sell well? Sometimes books don't sell well *at first*: very often a book will magically spring to life and go from a forgotten favorite to a phenomenon.

And so it's very important—if not essential—to think about writing as a long-term thing: a very long-term thing.   It's not just one (early) bestseller, but a life of book after book that will give you multiple chances at creating a career.

Besides, if you tailor your publicity to one book, then you'll have to restart the whole thing from scratch with the next one. If you instead think of exposure and publicity with regard to your entire body of work, then you can just add more books to the line, building momentum with each one. Publicity is damned hard—so why make it harder by having to do it over and over again?

The answer is that the first thing every writer should do when they finish one book, even before that book comes out, is to begin writing another one. Sure it's tough, trying to simultaneously write a book and create publicity for your entire life as a writer, but considering how much time it can sometimes take to establish your name, can you really afford to wait for sales that may not come? Why not take steps now and write a whole bunch of books?   Then just one has to be The One.   Besides, writing is something that gets better with practice, right? Not only will your next book be a good seller but, more importantly, it might be your best one—and if not that one, then the next, the next, the next ....

If this scenario scares you, and there's every reason it should, then remember that professional writing isn't done easily or quickly. But it *is* special, magical, and—most of all—takes a rare kind of bravery.

Never forget that.

CHAPTER 44: CRYSTAL BALLS

My Ouija board is warped, horoscopes don't include my planet, my tea is only instant and my entrails ... well, you don't want to know about my entrails.

These are certainly, absolutely, positively unsettling times to be anything, let alone a writer — and especially a erotica writer. But as I've said before, there's no reason to be frightened. Yes, there have been some big changes in writing and publishing and there are bound to be even more, but it's important for writers not only to try and work with this new world but also, believe it or not, to actually look forward to it.

I find it baffling that so many of my fellow writers, smut or not, are really digging their heels in over the ebook revolution. "Print or nothing!" seems to be their rallying cry. Well, not to speak ill of my friends or anything, but that kind of attitude will not get you anything but ... *nothing*. It's time to face facts, people: the old model of print publishing is gone — or might as well be gone unless you're on one of the *New York Times* bestseller lists.

That's not to say that print will ever really die. Books will always be here, but the way they are published and sold has changed — and is going to change even more.

As I teased in my intro a few paragraphs back, my powers of precognition are pretty weak, but here's my brief look at what might happen to the world of erotica writing and publishing in the next few years. I hope to show that the future may not be as scary as you think and that, in many ways, it will be better for all of us writers, erotica or non.

Bookstores are going to go bye-bye. Yeah, yeah, I know: there goes the smell of paper and all that nostalgic stuff. But face it: bookstores have never been writer-friendly, because they only have so much shelf space and unless you're a best seller, they simply can't afford to carry you.

That might have been a bit extreme. What I should have said is that *most* bookstores will vanish, because for most people, the Web will be the primary place for buying books. A few stores will remain, but either they will be places — like kiosks — where people can buy a paperback bestseller right then and there, or they will be showplaces for special edition books that are either not offered as digital editions (collector stuff) or as expanded editions that have features not found in their print versions. Think of an art gallery as opposed to an actual bookstore.

Print, as I've said — *ad nauseam* — will be pretty much gone. If you want to buy a book you'll either go to a publisher's site, a portal site — meaning a site dedicated to carrying books from a certain genre — or big stores like Amazon. There you will have a choice of options, and not just for the kind of ebook reader you use. You might see illustrated versions, or editions with animation. Others might feature a soundtrack, selected by the author to go along with their book. You may also see audio books, either the author or a performer reading or even the book done as a radio play with a whole ensemble of actors. There might be special editions with the author's notes included or even an earlier draft so you can see what was changed before the final version — kind of like margin notes. Or how about a version with hyperlinks, so you could click on any word or phrase or location and get more info about it?

If you want, you might be able to order a cheap paperback version of the book, or even a hardbound and illustrated version. If you don't like it, or get tired of it, you could send it back for a credit, the paper used in your hardcopy version getting recycled into someone else's.

What this means for writers is that the benchmark of having a publisher will become less and less important for getting your work out there. Many authors simply will decide to do it themselves. Now I do think that publishers — or a form of what publishers are now — will remain, if only to act as a marketplace for authors and to help with publicity and such. It also means that, except for a few rare exceptions, sales will be much lower. But this is actually a good thing: in the old days a book had to make a lot of money just to repay the cost of printing and shipping. With digital books — and print on demand — books don't need to make that much to show a profit.

Erotica, in this Brave New World I've been dreaming of, will no longer be ghettoized. A digital file can be created by, and sold by anyone. The problem will be dealing with huge outlets, and proprietary technology, like Apple's with its iTunes store. But as long as there are readers for ebooks available on any platform, then eBooks — of whatever subject matter — will be able to go wherever anyone wants them to go. And with print on demand, anyone can order anything anywhere.

I could be wrong about any of this — hell, I might even be wrong about all of this — but the point is that, as a writer, digging in your heels or covering your ears and going "lalalala" is not going to do anything but make you look silly or, at the very worst, leave you behind. Now is the time to seriously rethink what it means to be a writer. After all, just look at the basic nature of that word: a writer tells stories. We started doing it around a campfire, went to stone tablets then to papyrus, then to paper, then came the printing press, and now we have the Internet.

The future is here and it's time to welcome it — and the opportunities it may bring.

CHAPTER 45: THE END OF EROTICA? OR THE BEGINNING?

I want erotica to vanish, to disappear as a literary genre, to utterly and completely go away.

Am I biting the hand that's fed me? Sour grapes? Making noise for the sake of noise? It's none of the above, so hear me out.

Erotica exists because a need wasn't being met. Readers looked around at movies, books, television, and every other medium and noticed that something was missing. Rob and Laura Petrie had twin beds, and Ricky Ricardo and Lucy pulled off a trick not seen since Mary got knocked up by a ghost: a virgin (as far as we know) birth. If a book managed to actually talk about what happened behind closed doors and under the sheets, it was immediately banned, burned, or branded indecent.

So then came erotica: a peek behind those doors and under those covers. Sex was out in the open and, more importantly, it was profitable. Sex sold, and very well — and with anything that sells well, the people doing the selling began to make more and more and more of it.

That, in itself, isn't a bad thing. After all, if sex didn't sell we wouldn't have MTV, Fox, beer ads, Britney Spears, Ron Jeremy, the entire literary erotica genre, or even the Erotica Readers and Writers Association and my column. But all this and more is popular, and remains popular, because it doesn't exist anywhere else.

Pick up a book, switch on the tube, plop down half your paycheck for a movie ticket and sure there might be hints, suggestions, or allusions, but that'll be it.

Meanwhile, out here in the wild woolies of smut writing, we continue to write books and stories that address what no one else seems to be talking about: sex. The problem is that for the longest time, we were part of an opposite but equal problem, which was talking about nothing but sex.

Luckily, this has been changing. It used to be that just simply writing s-e-x was enough, but as the public started to get more, they also began asking for more. Editors, publishers and (more importantly) readers have responded by demanding erotica with depth, meaning, wit, style, and sophistication — and writers have been doing exactly that, pushing the boundaries of what sex writing can be.

The result? Erotica writers have created a genre worthy of respect and serious, non-genre attention. This is a great time to be working in this field, because for the first time writing about sex is not a guarantee of condemnation or exile to a professional Elba. Erotica writers are breaking out and otherwise mainstream publishers are beginning to pay serious attention to the marketability of sex. Because of what's developed in the genre, they can sell it without blushing.

This is a good thing for another, more important reason. It's crystal ball time: as erotica becomes more and more refined and mature, more elegant and accepted, it may very well begin to be accepted as a valid and respected form of literature. But what I really hope will happen is what's happened with many other genres: assimilation. It used to be that anything to do with time travel, aliens, or space travel was exiled to science fiction. Then came a renaissance in that genre, and a subsequent use of the old elements in new ways — Kurt Vonnegut comes immediately to mind. The same thing has happened with mysteries, horror, romance, comic books (excuse me, "graphic novels"), television, and so forth.

As the sexually explicit techniques and methods developed in erotica permeate other genres, the need for erotica as its own separate, unique place in bookstores will fade, and then vanish. Erotica will become what it always should have been: a part of life, legitimate and respected — not something to be ashamed of, hidden away, or even just separate.

How will that serve us in the erotica-writing world? Wonderfully, I think. Erotica is fun, and I definitely believe that, but it's only one genre. As we become better and better writers, trying new things, new techniques, and dipping our toes in new pools, other venues will open up, other — better — playgrounds to frolic in.

Sure it might be scary, once erotica merges with the rest of the world and fades away as a genre in its own right. But think of how much better that world will be, a place where sex is something to be talked about, celebrated, and understood without fear or shame.

Our genre may disappear, and could utterly and completely go away — but we will have accomplished something remarkable:

We changed the world.

ABOUT THE AUTHOR

M. Christian is an acknowledged master of erotica with more than 300 stories in such anthologies as *Best American Erotica, Best Gay Erotica, Best Lesbian Erotica, Best Bisexual Erotica, Best Fetish Erotica,* and many, many other anthologies, magazines, and Web sites. He is the editor of 20 anthologies including the *Best S/M Erotica* series, *The Burning Pen, Guilty Pleasures, The Mammoth Book of Future Cops* and *The Mammoth Book of Tales of the Road* (with Maxim Jakubowksi) and *Confessions, Garden of Perverse,* and *Amazons* (with Sage Vivant) as well as many others. He is the author of the collections *Dirty Words, Speaking Parts, The Bachelor Machine, Licks & Promises, Filthy, Love Without Gun Control, Rude Mechanicals,* and *Coming Together: M. Christian;* and the novels *Running Dry, The Very Bloody Marys, Me2, Brushes,* and *Painted Doll.* See www.mchristian.com for more information.

CPSIA information can be obtained at www.ICGtesting.com
Printed in the USA
BVOW011917150812

297985BV00001B/4/P

9 781615 083015